# PARTHENA'S PROMISE

1815: Parthena arrives in a small Yorkshire village to take up a post as governess, only to find that the family has moved away, leaving her stranded on her own in an unfamiliar place. Here she meets Jerome Fender, a soldier returning from the wars. He is enchanted by Thena and offers to help her. Full of desperation, however, she 'borrows' his money, shouting a promise to pay him back as she flees. Incensed, Jerome vows to find her and get his money back — as well as an explanation . . .

VALERIE HOLMES

# PARTHENA'S PROMISE

*Complete and Unabridged*

**LINFORD**
*Leicester*

First published in Great Britain in 2015

First Linford Edition
published 2017

A catalogue record for this book is available
from the British Library.

ISBN 978–1–4448–3126–9

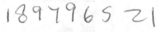

Published by
F. A. Thorpe (Publishing)
Anstey, Leicestershire

Set by Words & Graphics Ltd.
Anstey, Leicestershire
Printed and bound in Great Britain by
T. J. International Ltd., Padstow, Cornwall

This book is printed on acid-free paper

# SPECIAL MESSAGE TO READERS

**THE ULVERSCROFT FOUNDATION**
**(registered UK charity number 264873)**
was established in 1972 to provide funds for
research, diagnosis and treatment of eye diseases.
Examples of major projects funded by
the Ulverscroft Foundation are:-

- The Children's Eye Unit at Moorfields Eye Hospital, London
- The Ulverscroft Children's Eye Unit at Great Ormond Street Hospital for Sick Children
- Funding research into eye diseases and treatment at the Department of Ophthalmology, University of Leicester
- The Ulverscroft Vision Research Group, Institute of Child Health
- Twin operating theatres at the Western Ophthalmic Hospital, London
- The Chair of Ophthalmology at the Royal Australian College of Ophthalmologists

You can help further the work of the Foundation
by making a donation or leaving a legacy.
Every contribution is gratefully received. If you
would like to help support the Foundation or
require further information, please contact:

**THE ULVERSCROFT FOUNDATION**
**The Green, Bradgate Road, Anstey**
**Leicester LE7 7FU, England**
**Tel: (0116) 236 4325**

**website: www.foundation.ulverscroft.com**

# 1

## 1815

Breathing the fresh, cold air into his lungs, Jerome rested against the wall of the old inn. He could hear the drunken banter from within, the raucous laughter and shouts of men celebrating their freedom with the women. But to him, out here was a cacophony of peace. These noises were far away from the blasts of shot ripping through screaming bodies, of cannon or the cries of death. He rested his eyes a moment, trying to blank out the haunting visions he had seen. Instead he tried to focus on the familiar country smells of the North Yorkshire market town, to override the memories of burning smoke that seemed to cling to his nostrils, and the smell of blood and death. Gradually his senses seemed temporarily cleansed of the hatred that he had heard pouring out of men's mouths for the past five lonely years. It evaporated like his breath in the chilly air.

What was it the recruiting sergeant had told the young men he enlisted? 'A battlefield is where camaraderie and honour are at their highest'? No — it was a deafening, mind-blowing place, where a soul could be destroyed, as they had soon found out when the bodies fell at their sides. Jerome had been one of the 'lucky' ones, having survived. Now he longed for one thing only: to find his true love, a life-partner to cherish. Someone who would share his lonely moments, remove the pain of isolation, and fill his home with warmth. Someone, whoever and wherever she was, who would hold him like she needed him, and value him not just for his ability to hunt, skirmish and keep men in order, like the army had. She would *want* him — Jerome Fender. But that person would have to be very special, because more than anything he wanted to rekindle feelings in his heart again, not just survive by thinking with his head.

Was it too late? Had his heart hardened beyond a point where he was able to feel true love? Or was his head now cynical beyond the understanding of finer feelings? How would he ever keep a young maid interested in trivial conversation, when he had returned from war and remembered little of parlour games and the habits of polite society? Jerome only wanted to own and work his own small portion of land, growing crops to feed his family; it was a romantic notion, but one that had kept him sane between the insanity of battles. He loved this area, as it brought back childhood memories of growing up on their northern estate until they were made to leave to return for the season in London. He shook his head; he liked to breathe fresh air.

Now that he had set his task, he was going to find her, this elusive butterfly bride who would flutter into his life, love him for *who* he was and not *what* he was, and stay with him for the duration. He shook his head again and laughed. God, if his men knew what had become of their captain. Next he would be writing verse and reading the love sonnets of the great bards. At a time when so many men were returning to the country desolate, in an equally lonely or needier state than he, Jerome was fantasising about finding a soulmate. Some managed it, and some never could.

It was as he gazed up at the starlit sky, enjoying the moment of peace, that he realised even his own family would think him completely mad. His mother would possibly abandon him as the black sheep, and his younger brother would take delight in his great fall from grace as he stooped below his station to actually work the land. He was a returning hero, about whom his brother preached as if he idolised him — which ironically his God did not allow. However, Jules did not idolise his brother, but had been jealous since childhood of his spirit and place as the firstborn male.

Images of his mother sprang to Jerome's mind. She would never understand that, with his education and inheritance, he craved some peace: the time to settle and the ability to be at one with the land — not fight over it, but work it. It was in that moment, as a revelation broke through his thoughts of what he had considered was possibly the first signs of madness, when Jerome first saw her approaching.

The young maid walked towards him like a faerie in the night. She appeared to be light of foot, even if her feet were wearing a pair of boots. Not his 'butterfly', but certainly a sight to behold. Her fair hair was neatly swept into a bun at the nape of her neck, topped by a small bonnet barely covering the curls that threatened to escape from its side. Yet she held her head erect, not exactly confident, but strangely proud. She looked cold as she wrapped herself in an old shawl, which she nervously allowed to slip off her shoulder as she approached him, revealing a thin muslin dress beneath.

Jerome didn't want to be a part of the noise and bustle inside the inn, among the heady smells of the drunken gathering, although it was so different to the bedlam of war. He watched the maid approach with interest, taking in the slight yet curvaceous contours. His longing for a woman had definitely deepened. Was he so desperate for female company that at the first sight of any wanton wench his mind began to romanticise? He had definitely been away at war too long. He studied her and swallowed. How he yearned to hold a wife in his arms, knowing the fighting was definitely finished, and to experience the peace of being in his own home, safe and no longer alone. But it was a wife he sought, not a whore. He had a deep yearning that only a good woman could fill, not a fleeting tryst in the night.

He sighed and let out a slow breath. She was a pretty one, and fresh of face; definitely not a woman who had been working the night for long. He watched her as she crossed the cobblestone road to stand boldly not two feet from where he propped himself against the wall of the inn.

'What's your name?' he asked as she stopped and looked at him. Her words of reply formed a gentle mist as she spoke. She must be so very cold, he thought. He was cold himself, despite his lined greatcoat.

'Miss . . . I mean Thena, sir,' she said in a delicate voice. It was polite; gentle almost, not heavy with the rough drawl of a local inn wench as he had expected.

Under the glow of the oil lamp that swung gently in the breeze above the corner of the inn, which lit its name: The Hare and Rabbit, Jerome stared into the rich blue eyes of the woman who was before him. He glanced down at her lovely lips, the gentle line of her neck and the curve of her bosom as she breathed in deeply. The fabric of her bodice stopped his eyes falling upon what was moving rhythmically in and out beneath it; but he could soon correct that, he had no doubt, if he was inclined to pass a coin or two her way.

'Thena,' she repeated again.

Jerome looked at her, intrigued, as her face tilted up to meet his gaze, her eyes heavy-lidded, her cheeks flushed. She played the innocent maid well, he thought. But no wench approached a man in the street at this late hour of the night unless she was out to earn some pennies by selling her body to the highest taker. The little minx, he thought as she gently licked her lips and then nervously swallowed.

'You're new here, aren't you?' he asked.

'Here, sir? You are — ?'

'Mr Fender, Jerome Fender.' He smiled at her, wondering why she cared what his name was.

'I have only just arrived. I was promised work, but the family who was to employ me have moved on. I tried finding employment in the mill town, but it is full, as it has been taken by returning soldiers. And now . . . I have nothing, and I . . . ' Large, soulful eyes stared at him, obviously wanting him to offer charity, help, or perhaps a bed for the night.

'Oh, you'll have no trouble finding work in there, a beauty like you!' he said. 'I thought I hadn't seen you serving in the taproom before, so what are you doing out here in the cold of the night? You'd have plenty of offers inside. At least five more men returned today, and there'll be more tomorrow. You could be kept busy all night if you liked.' He was intuitively leaning forward so that his mouth was only inches from hers, their lips so near. He had spoken honestly, but her face showed her shock. Or was it genuine fear at what he had intimated? By the moonlight, her eyes almost glistened. With

9

tears, or the cold? he wondered.

'I need work. I have nowhere to go, and I thought that you, perhaps, were also looking for . . . ' She turned her head away, tantalisingly, teasingly, he thought; very clever, or stupidly naive. If only she knew his heart was no longer a soft, caring one. It had once taken in the plight of waifs and strays, but he had seen too many. The world was full of grieving lost souls, or so it seemed. Women left in captured villages. Wenches who followed their men across a continent in a war they had never imagined, to be widowed and left with little choice but to find another to care for them; or worse, take anyone who needed relief.

Jerome knew she had not entered the building. Perhaps she was hoping he would answer her silent plea to find herself another man. 'You have not asked for help inside yet?' Was she trying to find herself just one man? Perhaps she realised he was a soldier just returned who wanted a wench to keep his bed warm. Was that her game? If it was, then should he? Could he? But no, a temporary bedmate was not what he sought. Yet it would be a safer place for her to lay her head than taking her chances with any old ruffian off the street.

'No, sir. I was too scared, and I . . . ' She swallowed again, and he noticed that her hand was trembling slightly as she pulled her shawl back upon her shoulder.

'You meet some unsavoury characters out here. They're not all gentlemen.' He smiled and placed a hand on the wooden frame of the back door to The Hare and Rabbit.

'Like you, sir?' she said. An anxious tremble entered her voice. She was either genuinely in diminished circumstances or a damned good actress. Jerome was wondering which was true.

'What do you want? To whore yourself? Are you desperate?'

He heard her gasp and she instantly stepped backwards. It was then that two men pushed the door of the inn open with the force of their bodies as they continued their brawl out in the street. Jerome was momentarily knocked against the wench. He grabbed her shoulders and she his waist. They had to cling to each other in order to keep their balance and not fall in the fouled and muddied street. Jerome spun her around away from the doorway as onlookers poured out, jeering and egging the two drunken soldiers on. They would no doubt be battered and bruised by morning, but all men had had enough of killing this night. Their fight was just a brawl.

'I'm sorry,' Thena said as she clung to him, his coat forming a layer of warmth around them, trapping their body heat inside.

'It was not your fault.' He still held on to her shoulders as he looked down at her anxious eyes. She steadied her body against his, but straightened as soon as she regained her balance and composure. She left a void in her place in the cool of the night air, as Jerome somewhat reluctantly let her go. Then she quickly grabbed her shawl, which had slipped to the ground; her hands clung to it as she took another step away. She wrapped it tightly around her slight frame and backed further off. Her eyes fixed on his; she hardly blinked as he held her gaze. Beautiful eyes: they were striking even in the poor light of the moon and the lamp, yet he knew not why.

He saw her mouth moving before he realised she was trying to tell him something. He saw her swallow as she hesitated before completing whatever it was she intended to tell him, but the noise of the brawl almost drowned out her words.

'What did you say?' he asked. She blinked, but did not reply. 'Do you want to go inside? I will get you some food, and we can talk away from this commotion,' he shouted as she continued her retreat. 'You do not need to fear me. I can help you.' He heard the words coming from his mouth and had no idea why they should. Why would he help her? The air must be addling his wits; or perhaps it was his loneliness getting the better of him.

'No . . . I'm sorry,' she shouted back to him. 'I will repay your kindness . . . I promise!' she managed to shout above the baying crowd nearby as the fight continued in the muddied street.

'Wait!' he yelled. A cheer went up as one man lay face down in the dirt, groaning. The other had his hands raised high. Jerome could not cross the street after Thena, as part of the group jostled to return to their drinks. When the crowd finally cleared, it was too late: she had turned and run away, lost in the darkness of the night.

Jerome hesitated. For a moment he was going to follow her, or at least try to, by running in the direction she had gone. But another crowd of revellers had spilled onto the road and had grown in number, blocking his way and the vision of his little faerie friend.

The man who had appeared to have been knocked out cold stood up in a blur of confusion and hit out at another who was not his opponent. A new fight ensued, only this time others joined in. After some moments, the two-man fight spread to six, eight, and more. Jerome tired of it all and went back inside the inn.

Whoever this Thena was, she was gone, and perhaps it was for the better. He could not take on the cause of every deserted wench: they were many, as were the widows and the young lovers whose men would never return to them — or if they did, never as they were in mind and body before they went to war. Jerome decided that he may as well sleep off the last of this strange evening and plan what he should do in the morning when he had a clearer head.

The problem he faced was a simple question: should he go back to the 'civilised world' of London to have his mama scout for a suitable match for him, or find a woman he could truly love by himself? He would think on it — or rather sleep upon it.

* * *

But the morning shone no more light on his predicament, as the day was dull and grey. Rain would come soon and be heavy, he decided. It was only when he put his coat on and prepared to venture out, curious to see if the faerie of the night reappeared in the daylight hours, that he realised his coin purse was missing.

He glanced around the room, on the small side-table, in his bag, on the window seat, but could not see it. He sighed and tried to retrace what he had done the evening before in his mind. Jerome thought hard, and clearly remembered standing outside the inn gazing at the stars with his hand in his pocket holding the purse as he considered what he truly wanted in life. Then he remembered the woman coming to him, like a vision. Next the fight broke out, pushing the inn door open wide with a clout that bound him and the faerie together in his arms. He definitely remembered the warmth they shared — and then the realisation dawned upon him. What was it she shouted into the night — ? Yes, of course; her words made sense now: *I will repay your kindness . . . I promise!* She promised!

'The little bitch!' he spat out, and knew instantly what he would do next.

# 2

Thena kept running until she was beyond the town and climbing the steep path that led onto the moor road. Once atop, she knew what she was looking for: an ancient milestone. This was the place where she would find the open moor trods to the village in the next dale. She had to keep moving because the cold bit into her skin, but the stars and the moon lit her way clearly enough. She knew the path well from her childhood. It would take her an hour, maybe a little more, but if she hurried she would be there before the night froze over and she perished.

Thena used to help the sisters move their produce from the gardens at the school to the abbey in Gorebeck. There, they and a few of the other girls in their care would rest and spend the night before heading back the next day to the school, where they would tend the gardens and mend and make things for the nuns to sell on again and sustain the work they did. In between, Thena was taught basic lessons. Her education had been unusual at the abbey school, but she had learned so many useful skills that she did not care. Her father had taken a very different view of things, however, when she was finally allowed home in the summer and told him of the things she had learnt to do. He decided a more refined finishing school was required, and so she was moved away. Thena had pined for her days outdoors, helping the nuns and being at one with the country.

After taking Mr Fender's coin purse, she had collected her bag from its hiding place behind the stable and made her immediate escape. Momentarily stopping to pour the coins onto her hand, to discover how large the debt was that she would need to repay him, Thena was shocked. She had expected no more than a few shillings, not crowns. She gasped. You could be hanged or transported for less — a lot less. With renewed urgency in her stride, she had headed straight for the trods. She knew it was daring or foolish to risk the path across the moors. What if the stone had been reused and moved? However, being caught was not an option she could consider.

She increased her pace as she left the village, realising she could be hunted by the hounds unless she could disappear and find a way of using the money to leave the area quickly. As she walked, she quelled the panic inside her by planning how she would take up a respectable position, perhaps start her own small enterprise to recapture her previous position in life. She was on open moorland and prayed that the rains, wind or frost did not set in. She had to keep moving at speed to stay warm, control her fear, and make this crossing more quickly than she had ever done before. Praying with all her heart as she went — for a child's memory can play the adult's false — she hoped this journey was a shorter one than she remembered.

Now, though, as she faced the open expanse of moorland, her immediate need was to keep herself warm. Taking out her pelisse from her bag, she put it on and wrapped her shawls over the top of her bonnet and her shoulders for extra protection against the night air. With now-gloved hands, Thena carried her bag and continued along the stone pathway that ancient monks, long since dead, had used before her.

She hummed songs and recited texts from the Bible to herself — anything to keep her mind and body from numbing. The irony of doing so was not lost on her, as she had broken one commandment — that of not stealing — which she never would have thought possible of herself. Now she prayed that she would be able to repay the man and that she would never have to break another commandment. She was, admittedly, a sinner; but her cousin Bertram had been one first. He had lied to her and sent her on a wild goose chase in order to rid himself of the obligation of providing a home for her. She would see justice done.

If her father was looking down on his errant daughter now, what would he think of her? She chose to be called a thief rather than becoming a whore! Why was she in these desperate straits, anyway? Because he had not seen fit to trust a female with her own money settled upon her, and so had allowed Bertram to squander it at will and send Thena halfway up the country to take a governess's position that did not even exist! Thank God in heaven, Thena thought, that she had been initially educated at a school in the same area, or she would have been totally lost.

Thena's blood slowly began to boil. Her inner warmth was now generated by anger, her cousin's betrayal, and the need to regain what the law would not acknowledge was hers. But how? She sighed, tears of frustration stinging her eyes. She would have to be patient to achieve any form of justice. First she needed to survive, and that meant having money. She only hoped that Mr Fender did not realise what she had done and instead blamed the man who had jostled them as the fight broke out. He would not be able to identify the culprit because he had been watching the fight and was pushed by the crowd.

She hadn't meant to become a thief, but what was better — to steal to survive, or to let men . . . No! She was worth more than that. It was not to be considered. Was that what cousin Bertram had hoped would happen to her?

For a solitary moment, when Mr Fender had fallen against her, Thena had been lost in the warmth of his coat and realised how near she was, because she had even thought of hugging him longer: the touch of another human, one who was being kind and seemingly caring, had appealed. Yes, for a split second she had considered doing the unthinkable and offering herself up like some form of sacrifice. At that point, however, she had seen his valuable fob watch, which reminded her of the life she had enjoyed before her father had died only a year ago. Thena could never hope to recapture it, not as a young woman from a good family; but she could make money herself. She had an enterprising spirit, and had seen how the nuns made things to create funds. She could do that, and train young girls also. If she threw herself at the first decent man she found in the street, what would become of her?

So she would rather become a thief, just once, just to make a new start. She had taken the man's coin but left his wallet, fob watch and chain, looking upon the purse as a loan she would promise to repay him. He was Mr Jerome Fender; she'd find him once things were sorted out.

She stopped for a fleeting moment and stared at the stars. 'I will return what I have stolen and find justice!' she whispered with feeling. 'I promised, and Parthena does not break her word!' Then as her body shivered, she continued again at speed. So long as she kept to the flagstone pathway, she would find her way back to the abbey; they would give her shelter for a small gift that she could now offer them. But if she ventured off this ancient path, she would be lost in the bog, and no one would ever find her. Then Mr Fender would never be reunited with his money.

# 3

Jerome rose early and saddled his horse. He had a clear head, unlike most of the occupants of the inn from the night before. They were either bruised, still drunk, or recovering from their exertions. A few broken stools had been thrown into the street, the evidence of the night's brawl. Before he left, he scouted the town for the young woman — the faerie of the night. The blacksmith was up early and working, so Jerome asked about her, describing her as best he could, and surprised that he had to withhold details like the colour of her eyes and the curve of her lips.

'Aye, I saw her in the street yesterday, then last evening, looking a sight anxious about something, but I don't know no more.' He hammered a piece of metal on his anvil and then paused, mallet raised. 'Ah yes — she asked about a house. It had been sold on, and the people she was looking up were long gone. So I suggested that she go to the mill and ask for work there. I thought they might take her on, but as I said, I saw her last evening looking edgy like, so perhaps she found no luck there either.' He smashed the hammer down then turned around and forced the metal into the flames, using his other hand to work the bellows. He was now engrossed in his business, and Jerome had no wish to come between him and his task.

So the mill would be the next place Jerome would visit in his quest for information about his faerie of the night, who in actuality had turned out to be more of a wanton witch. If he could discover her identity and where she came from, he would be able to trace her easily enough. Perhaps there was a desperate tale behind her actions, like so many people had to tell, though that was no excuse to thieve from someone who would have offered her at least a warm meal and a bed for the night.

He rode out the two miles to the watermill. This one querned no flour; it had weaving machines in it. Cotton was no longer a cottage industry in the area, where flax was spun and woven into lengths of cloth by families in their homes. The manufactories were doing remarkably well at replacing them by providing vast quantities of cloth in one place. This was the future of the industry, and it was one that had a harsh reality to it for the men, women and children who worked there as the human cogs of this new process driven by noisy machines. People either praised the new manufactories as places of vast progress and profit, or saw them as fodder for a revolution to the cotton industry, hated for the demise of the local traditions and employment. Many of those who left their homes to work long, hard hours in such a noisy place lost their community and the sense of belonging that went with it. Still, it was a lot better than the workhouse, Jerome thought.

He rode to the edge of the town and took a road that led to where the river flowed quite fast as it descended through the village. It was not the biggest mill he had ever seen, but as he approached he could already hear the clattering of machinery, see the smoke from the chimney, and watch as bales were placed onto long, low boats to carry them into town where they would be transported by wagons to the River Ouse and on to York. All was busy as he entered through the ornate iron gates where the name 'Beckton Cotton Mill' proclaimed proudly what it was. Jerome tethered his horse's reins to a hook outside what looked to be the main offices. A sturdy man was busy at his employment as Jerome approached his desk. The room was sparse of furniture beyond his own counter and the many files and drawers that surrounded him on three walls.

'What can I do for you, sir?' the man behind the counting desk asked as he stared at Jerome through his monocle.

Jerome smiled. He had no wish to antagonise the chap, as he needed information, and had no real reason he could give as to why he was there and had not instead summoned the constable to report the theft. 'I am trying to find the young woman who came here yesterday seeking work,' he said.

The portly man looked at him and removed the glass. 'We had three young women arrive yesterday and two the day before. These are hard times, sir. Which one is it you seek?'

Jerome described her as best he could without trying to sound as if he was infatuated by her eyes, her innocent demeanour and her thieving hands. 'Slight of build, wearing a shawl and bonnet, and about five feet in height. She has striking eyes.' The last comment surprised him; it slipped out. Had she bewitched him? Why he should have remembered such a thing when he was describing a cutpurse, he did not know. To be fair, though, she was hardly a cutpurse in the sense of what you'd find in the Seven Dials of London. No, she was an opportunist and a little minx. However, if he brought her before a magistrate, her sentence would be the same. Jerome was not ready to cast her to the wolves before finding her himself and demanding at least a half-decent reason as to what she was about.

'Aye, sir, there was a pretty little thing came here yesterday in a bit of a flummox. Claimed she had expected to be a governess for a respectable family, but that correspondence had been delayed and she had missed their departure, or some such tale. For a family in one of them big new houses in town. I'll admit she spun her words well enough to be credible, and knew how to talk fine, but what use is a governess in a mill where graft is menial and hours long? They'd laugh at her as she tripped over every stray bobbin. I could offer her nothing other than my condolences and good wishes for another position to turn up, and so she left.' He shrugged and replaced his monocle.

'Did she give you her name, or where she was staying?' Jerome hoped to at least learn that much.

The man sighed. 'I am not sure of it. Why do you wish to know?' He looked at him curiously. 'How is it that you do not know for whom you seek?'

Jerome did not know why he had not called her a thief and have her hounded by the law, other than perhaps it was a matter of personal pride. He would hunt her down himself; then she would pay him back in coin and labour until she learnt her lesson. If there was to be a trial, he would present her before it himself, if he thought she was deserving of a harsher punishment. But for now he just wanted to find her and teach her a lesson she would not forget. If she had tried it on many a gentleman of his acquaintance, no mercy would be shown by them, and an example set. He had hunted Napoleon's Voltigeurs, so how difficult could it be to catch one slip of a woman on the run?

'I am trying to help her, but first I need to find her.' He stared at the man. It was not a lie, for he had every intention of showing her the error of her ways, and in so doing he would help her to be a better person. He almost smiled; but remembering the money she had taken from him without him even realising it kept any humour from his lips. Had she not felt the wallet in his pocket? If she had taken that, he would have raised the hunting hounds himself from their kennels and set them on her. The coin purse was a big enough loss, as it had sufficient to keep her off the streets for months. Still, he had been mesmerised by those eyes, and lost in his thoughts of finding a soulmate. Deluded by his dreams and distracted by the street fight, he had not even felt the weight of his purse being lifted from his pocket.

The man's voice brought him out of

his momentary reverie. Realising how much he could have lost had made finding Thena more crucial rather than less. 'Munro,' the man said. 'Miss Munro. That is all I know of her. I am a busy man, sir, and she has to find her own way in life, as we all do. Good day to you.' His head turned back down as his focus returned to the letter he had been writing. Then he looked up suddenly, as if a thought had just struck him. 'A word of advice, sir. If you don't mind my being so bold?'

Jerome stopped in half-turn as he was about to walk away, intrigued by what advice this man could offer him. 'Go on.'

'There are many tales of heartbreak waiting to be heard, and each begging for help. But if you help one, word gets around, and then how are you going to help them all? Believe me — walk on by, especially from the ones with striking eyes. They act like lures to decent folk. Wenches will always find themselves a warm bed. Worry more for the men who cannot find work after risking their lives fighting Boney abroad.' He nodded and then continued working.

Jerome did not bother to respond. He had a name — Miss Thena Munro — and knew her description, but nothing else. How then to catch his elusive, light-fingered faerie?

The town had a road leading east to Gorebeck, the old market town where the crossroads met to the north, the south, the coast to the east, this village where he now was, or further west, which would lead across the Yorkshire Dales to the Pennines. He rode to the junction and stopped for a moment. She could not take wings and fly. The moors were treacherous and no doubt impassable unless you were a sheep or a shepherd, so she would have to take to the road. Instinct told Jerome to head for Gorebeck. It was nearer, and from there she could pay her way on a coach. If she had done so, he'd have her, because his horse could go faster than any dragging such a burden behind them. He breathed in the morning air and smiled. The hunt had begun. His senses had not let him down so far — they had saved his life many times; but the difference now was that he had all the time in the world to find a faerie thief, and with no Voltigeurs hunting him.

★ ★ ★

Daylight broke as Thena made her way down the track from the moors towards the abbey at the southern edge of the town. It nestled amongst a small woodland, sheltered from the wind and on three sides by high ground leading to the moor above. You could easily pass by and not even know the place existed, which was most likely how it had survived when so many others in the region, like Rievaulx, Whitby and Byland, lay in ruins.

Exhausted, she almost stumbled through the gates into the well-tended gardens that supplied the nuns with what they needed and also the excess to sell. Nothing seemed to have changed in the twelve years since she was last there. Hoping on hope that Mother Ursula still ruled the order, Thena made her way to the large wooden door with the heavy knocker on it and announced her presence. It seemed an age before someone came, but when they did the door that she had not realised she had been leaning on gave way and Thena made her entrance. The nun screamed as she fell at her feet. Embarrassed, Thena tried to apologise, but her world spun and she blacked out. Thena had arrived, and with the feeling of safety came the realisation that she had spent her final reserves of energy.

# 4

Jerome's mood was as bleak as the weather as he rode into Gorebeck. No one was on the streets as the rain lashed down. 'God in Heaven!' he swore as he stared at the steeple of the Norman church by the stone bridge that crossed the narrow river, as he struggled against the strong northeasterly wind. 'I thought rain fell from the sky, not drove across the country horizontally!' he muttered the last few yards. Holding onto his hat with one hand, he steered the horse towards the shelter of the stabling at the back of an inn. It was too bleak to read the sign as it swung in the gusts of wind, but as he approached the buildings a lad came out and offered to take the reins. Jerome released his bag and ferreted inside for his other coin purse and passed the lad one. 'Tend him well!' Jerome shouted over the sound of a crack of thunder. The lad nodded as he led the horse away.

Jerome burst into the inn with a greater sense of purpose than he had intended to. The weather was foul, and so was his mood. Heads turned as he ducked below a beam. He stopped momentarily, removed his dripping hat, and waited for his eyes to acclimatise to the gloom. Faces stared at him from their cosy dry seats of stools or settles. Ignoring them, he walked straight over to the serving hatch, adding more water to the already soiled threshing that covered the flagstone floor.

'Best of the day, sir!' the serving wench greeted him. 'I'm Mary. What can I get for you?' Her smile was only spoiled by her browning teeth and strong breath.

'I think the best of the day is yet to come — I hope.' He smiled back at her, trying to lift his mood. 'A room with a tub would be fine, but first I need a good brandy.'

Mary winked at him and pulled a bottle of French brandy out from under the counter and poured him a decent measure. Jerome knew full well it was contraband, but he was not going to complain. He wanted to feel the mellow taste glide down his throat and warm his innards.

'Sally, make a room ready for the gentleman and have young Jeb fill up a tub for him by a warm fire,' Mary shouted without looking around, her eyes fixed instead on Jerome's wet, cold figure. There was a flurry of activity behind her as the lass and lad appeared from the back storeroom and went about their chores. 'Anything else?' Mary asked, obviously happy to have some new custom on this miserable, gloomy day.

Jerome glanced around the poky room and saw the locals take up their drinks and continue their conversations. Apparently he was not interesting enough to hold their attention. Good, he thought. He downed his drink in one and was grateful for it. 'Yes, you can help me further.' He looked at her and leaned nearer, wanting to keep his quest his own concern. 'I'm looking for a woman.'

Mary raised her brows. 'We run a respectable house here,' she said, and blinked as coyly as her life-hardened eyes were able to. She then leaned forward to meet his gaze; her bosom seemed to swell as she rested it on her arms, exposing more of her cleavage than he wished to see. 'However, for the right price we can arrange . . . most things . . . '

Jerome half-smiled, realising that in his intention not to have his faerie warned of his presence and take flight, he must have sounded like he was wanting a wench for the night. Looking at the hopeful eyes of the 'mature' woman who flirted with him now, it was all he could do not to swallow back his words and run. 'Sorry, I misled you . . . unintentionally of course. I meant that I am looking for a specific woman.'

'Another drink, sir?' Mary asked, standing straight again and holding the bottle up, waving it slightly.

'Yes, and a hot meal would be welcome after my tub. Now, I am looking for a young woman by the name of Miss Munro. She came ahead on her own, as I was delayed, and I was rather hoping that she may have already taken a room here.' He smiled and held his glass out for another drink, knowing that Mary would have some more coin from him one way or the other before she was willing to help him. If she could, that was. It was unlikely that his faerie would have gone unnoticed if she had turned up in such a place. Mary poured him another brandy and he drank it, realising how much he also needed food in his stomach; it was empty.

'Sorry, sir, no woman is staying here by that name or any other. We have a couple of officers, a mill owner and a priest. They're all waiting for the coach to York, but none have a single woman with them.'

'When will that leave?' Jerome asked.

'Tomorrow, midday. But it's fully booked, so there will be no space for her on that. If she's in town, she'll be easily spotted.' His face must have showed his disappointment. 'Mind, she may well have gone to the abbey for a bed. Depending on what sort of lady she is.' She winked. 'The more virtuous kind don't tend to stay on their ownsome in an inn. Is she virtuous?' she asked cheekily.

Jerome thought of the thieving little minx that had caught his attention and also his coin, and decided the word may fit her demeanour, but not her actions. Still, desperate people did desperate things. Right now he wanted warm food and a bath — and to get his hands on the virtuous woman he was chasing.

'Could you make enquiries for me?' he asked.

'Don't think I'd go near a place like that! I'd be struck down!' Mary laughed; a raucous coarse noise that made Jerome smile to hide the cringe he felt inside his cold and hungry gut.

'I may well be a bit obvious myself,' he said.

'Well . . . ' Mary glanced at the ceiling and sucked her browning teeth as she rubbed her thumb and forefinger together.

Jerome placed another coin on the counter and kept a finger upon it before she could pick it up. 'Are there any other inns in the town?' he asked.

'Aye, one at the other end. I doubt she would go there, though. I mean, it's positively ancient. Wooden floors warping, and the damn place falling apart around the guests' ears; not like our establishment here. This one's built to last.' She smiled at him.

Jerome realised that her competitor must still do quite well, or the place would not have survived if it was of the old timbered buildings from Shakespeare's time or before. This woman was cunning, he thought. 'You make a good point.' He released the coin. 'Have someone make enquiries discreetly, and let me know where she is if she has arrived in town. I will double this amount if you locate her,' he said.

'Good as done, mister.' Mary winked at him again.

Jerome nodded and then took his weary body up the rickety stairs to his room. He would take his rest, warm up and eat; then, when the rain ceased, he would see if anyone had found out where Thena was. If not, then before he left the place he would take a walk through the town, look out for her, and ask if she had been seen anywhere, including in the old inn.

His horse needed to rest and dry out as much as he did, but his determination to capture the wench had grown with every uncomfortable hour he had passed in the saddle, and in the driving rain. He was used to harsh conditions, but never had he been so easily duped. He had been foolish, but he was no man's or woman's fool. Thena would pay dearly. Would she have the gall to stay at an abbey? Would she go and repent of her sins? Would they take his money from her and lock the foolish girl away until she was old and bent over, and her life gone along with her beauty?

Well, why should he care what happened to her? He wanted his coin, and that would be the end of it . . . but for those memorable eyes.

\* \* \*

Thena awoke in a cold stone cell, huddled under two thick woollen blankets. The mattress she was lying on felt lumpy but warm, no doubt stuffed with remnants of wool, cotton and whatever other fabrics the sisters could spare to shred. At least it was not stuffed with hay like the abbey school ones had been in her time there. Girls slept two to a bed, with one blanket between them in a dormitory for twenty. There was much Thena had enjoyed about her school days, but not the nights in winter.

She saw the chamber pot sticking out from under her bed as she sat up, and was careful how she used it. Once satisfied, she cringed, remembering the communal buckets of the dormitory. Deciding she had had enough of nostalgia, she combed out her hair, swept it into a bun and placed her bonnet atop it, then made sure her possessions had not been tampered with. Her boots had been cleaned and left on the floor for her by a stool, atop which was her coat.

She smiled even wider at the gesture of care. How lovely it was to see the sign of another person's effort on her behalf. There was a time when she had a maid to come when called, who she thought of as her possession, with no life or will of her own, just paid to serve. What a price was paid for her comfort. Now Thena was a different person, and saw the value in every small aspect of life. In fact, she now saw the value of life itself. Never again would she complain of being bored. The poor, apparently, had no right to be bored, tired, ill or ambitious. She was not used to being poor and had no intention of being so again.

Dismissing the source of her money, she pulled on her coat and boots and collected her bag. It was only when she tried to open the door that she found it to be locked. She felt an overwhelming rush of fear and panic. Had she been found out already? Had the man come looking for his coin? In that moment she valued nothing more than the one thing that had just been taken from her — her freedom. She hammered on the door. She knew how thick the walls were and how long the corridor was. She heard feet running toward her cell and grabbed her bag. With her stolen guineas, she had no reason to doubt why she had been locked in. If they knew . . .

She swallowed and tried to think quickly of a plausible way to explain her actions. If the man Fender had found her, her life could be forfeit for her crime. She now wished she had just run to the sisters in the first place and begged for their help; but how to undo what she had done in desperation? They might make her join the order. If she told them the truth now, she had no doubt they would put the money to good use and have her there repenting from now until her dotage.

Thena was not prepared for that. She would have to find Mr Fender and repay him, but she could not presently face the long trek back across the moor. Her head swam, she had not eaten, and her thirst was great also. She clung to her bag as the door opened; her mouth felt dry, and the room moved around her. She was fortunate that as two sisters entered the room, they realised she was about to fall and grabbed her quickly, stopping her from bashing her head on the stone floor.

'My dear!' one exclaimed as she was steadied. 'Come with us. You have rested but now need to eat.'

Thena agreed. She felt light-headed and heavy-hearted. She was led to where the sisters were having their broth and bread in a neat row at a table in the centre of an old stone arched room. The vaulted ceiling seemed high and the air around her cold. No one spoke, but she was escorted to an empty space and a sister gestured that she should be seated. Still with her bag close by her feet, Thena climbed in as smoothly as she could. She took little persuasion to consume the warm food, and as it slipped down her throat she felt her energy return as if it was the nectar of life that she had imbibed. Gratefully, without looking around or speaking, she finished her meal, using her bread to leave her bowl clean.

'You must come with me now,' a nun said to her, and stepped back ready for Thena to stand. No one else spoke. They silently stacked their plates as she left. Eyes watched her, but no one gestured or smiled. It was as if she was a foreigner who had invaded their space, and they were wary of her. They did not know what to make of her. Perhaps that was as she seemed to them — a threat; someone who did not follow their rules; an outsider.

Thena followed her escort around the stone corridor to the corner of a quadrangle, the middle of which was being used to grow small crops of herbs within the sheltered walls. An older nun hoed it lovingly, focused on her task. The place had a strange feeling of peace about it that stilled Thena's anxious heart. They stopped where a flight of stairs spiralled up out of sight behind the ancient wall. Here the nun stepped aside again and allowed Thena to climb them first. She thought of refusing, fearing it could be a trap; but she also wanted to see if it was the same Mother Ursula, the mother superior from her childhood, who sat in the office above. How old would she now be? Thena wondered. She followed the curve of the stone wall, carefully placing her feet on the small worn steps that had had many a footfall upon them over the centuries. When she came to a wooden door, she knocked and waited momentarily until a strong voice ordered, 'Come in!'

Thena placed her free hand on the large iron handle, her other still clinging to her bag with the stolen coin hidden inside. She swallowed, almost feeling as if the sin of her crime could be read in her eyes as she entered. Peace had vanished again, and guilt gnawed at her heart instead.

The room was stark. A woman sat behind a desk on a simple chair. There was no fire in the hearth behind her, and no hangings covered the bare stone walls. The wooden floor creaked as Thena crossed its uneven surface.

The woman watched her, but did not speak until Thena stood before her. 'Your name, girl,' she said.

'I am sorry to have inconvenienced you, and would like to offer you a — '

'Do you have a problem hearing me

or comprehending my questions, girl? I asked you what your name is.'

'Yes, I heard well enough. I was going to offer you a donation before I left.' Thena looked at the hard face of the woman opposite her. This was not the gentle old lady she had seen as a child. She did not care for the woman's tone, her dominant manner, or her assertion that Thena had to obey her like one of her order.

'Who are you running from, girl?' she continued.

'Would half a crown be sufficient for your kindness and hospitality?' Thena pressed. She decided the sooner she left, the better. She was beginning to feel trapped, and had no wish to be incarcerated here or in a gaol. As quickly as she could, she put her hand inside her bag and found the coin she sought, which she offered up for the woman to take.

Instead, the mother superior slowly sat back in the chair and stared at her. 'We are giving you room and board free of charge. But we are not running a boarding house here, or a shelter for waifs and strays as they pass by. I take it from this you have no wish to join our order as a novice.'

Thena swallowed. She nearly dropped the bag at the thought, and the desire to take to her heels and run was very strong. 'I merely sought shelter. If it was freely given, then I thank you for your charity and ask that you accept this as a donation so that you can help a waif or stray who needs help and who is unable to offer payment of any kind.'

'So tell me who it is who turns up desperate at our door in the daylight hours, and then offers to pay handsomely for our hospitality.' She gestured that Thena should leave the coin on the desk.

'I would bid you good day,' Thena answered and turned to leave, but her exit was blocked by a nun, whose ample figure all but filled the width of the doorway. She made no attempt to move, but folded her arms and stared at Thena. One finger gestured that she should turn around and face the mother superior.

Thena felt intimidated. She wanted to protest, but the last thing she needed was more trouble or suspicion thrown upon her. Although this interview was not going well, perhaps she had used the wrong tone. 'I merely wish to leave and trouble you no further,' she said to the mother superior, and smiled. 'You have not given me your name, either.' She stared back at the woman.

'You never asked, but my name is Mother Marisa, and I merely wish to know who it is that has slept under our roof in my care and who now wishes to leave in such a hurried fashion.' She leaned forward, her voice slightly gentler, but the look in her eyes as intense.

'My name is Miss Parthena Munro. Now may I leave?' Thena held the woman's gaze, but cursed her own stupidity — she had given her real name, without thinking. But then, this was a house of God. How could she lie and expect Him to protect her as she bumbled along on her present path of folly?

'Whence did you come, and why did you not go to the inn for rooms with such coin in your purse?' Mother Marisa studied her with a set expression that revealed her curiosity.

Thena realised that the nuns had most likely looked carefully through her bag, so Mother Marisa would know if she was telling the truth or lying to her face. 'I had an unfortunate experience. I was supposed to take a position as a governess, but found that the family had moved on by the time I arrived. Messages and letters had apparently crossed. I was left with nowhere to stay and nowhere to find suitable alternative accommodation.' Thena thought she saw a flicker of amusement in the woman's eyes, but she was unsure. If she had read the letter of introduction in Thena's belongings, then she knew

Thena was telling the truth, at least about that.

'This family was here in Gorebeck?' the sister in the doorway persisted.

Thena did not bother to turn around; she answered the woman's question directly to the mother superior. 'No, it was a respectable household over in the village of Beckton, in Beckton Dale.'

'You cannot have walked all this way by road. Who gave you a lift? A passing farmer?' Mother Marisa leaned forward. 'Have you any idea of the danger you put yourself in? Could you not use your money to catch a coach to wherever you originally hailed from?'

Thena looked at her and decided she was in the best place to make a giant leap of faith. She would tell the truth — almost. 'I walked over the old trods from Beckton to Gorebeck. I was at the abbey school as a child, and crossed the moors when the supplies were taken to market. I'd remembered it from then.' She watched as the mother superior stood to her full height, graceful and elegant in her poise. Although slight of build, she gave off such inner peace and confidence that Thena could only admire her and wish she had such poise herself.

'So you say you were in Beckton. You did not find the employment you expected, and from there moved on.' She was staring out of the window, apparently deep in thought or mulling over the information she had just been given.

'Yes, it is as I said.' Thena was beginning to feel quite anxious and slightly vexed. They had no right to keep her here.

'No more?' The woman looked at her.

'No more what?' Thena snapped, and instantly regretted her haste.

'You have nothing else to tell me, Miss Munro? Nothing else you would ask of me? Am I correct in assuming you have no intention of staying here?' She looked at Thena with a resigned expression that was in such a contrast to her original greeting, Thena wondered why she should change so.

'I wish to leave,' Thena stated emphatically.

'Very well,' Mother Marisa said, and nodded to the sister behind Thena, who opened the door wide.

'Thank you,' Thena said. But before she could take two steps, a gentleman entered the room, and she froze.

'You know this man?' Mother Marisa asked, her voice suggesting that Thena should think carefully before answering the question.

Thena swallowed. It seemed she had been caught easily as punishment for her sin. 'This is Mr Jerome Fender,' she began. 'I met him once only, but he has saved me from a fate worse than any I have previously encountered in my life. I owe him a great debt of gratitude.' She stood up straight and tried to keep the wobble from her voice as her body trembled.

'You are indeed fortunate, for this gentleman has told me he has travelled all this way seeking you out so that he can help you in your plight.' Mother Marisa looked sceptical, but stayed polite.

Thena stared at Mr Fender, wondering if there was a game of words being played out around her, or if he had really not told the sisters that she had stolen from him. Perhaps, she thought, she should tell them herself, because if they gave her sanctuary then he couldn't have her arrested, if that was his motive. 'Have you really travelled all this way to find me, Mr Fender?' she asked. 'Is it indeed your intention to help me by putting right the grievous wrong that has been done to me, and has seemingly drawn you into it as well?'

'I would be most interested to hear of this grievous wrong,' he answered, 'but perhaps we could leave the sisters in peace to their devotions whilst we ascertain the depth of your problems. I do not see any point in involving them further,' he added, not taking his eyes from hers. 'Do you?'

'Is this your wish, Miss Munro?' the mother superior asked.

'I should not bother you further,' Thena replied. Her head and her heart were giving her conflicting advice.

'Once you leave here, you are beyond the protection and the sanctuary of the abbey and my power.' She then addressed Jerome. 'Mr Fender, you must swear to me that you will take care of this lady and see that she is safe from harm. Whatever her circumstances, I believe they are not of her making, and would ask that a secure place of employment or a safe home be found for her.'

'I will see to it that she is well cared for and that any wrongs done to her are righted.' He looked straight at Thena. 'You have my oath on that, lady.'

'Then leave with my blessing.' Mother Marisa waved her hand and the nun opened the door wide. The time for talk had ended; now Thena had to step out into the world with the man whom she had robbed.

# 5

The minute they stepped outside the abbey grounds, Jerome cupped her elbow with his hand and removed her bag.

'Unhand me!' Thena protested.

He spun her around to face him, and one word stilled her: 'Silence!' She glared at him and was about to rebuke him further for manhandling her, but he shook his head slowly at her. 'Say one word, Miss Munro, and I will call in the local militia — their billet is not far away, and you are a common thief! Or I could find out where the local magistrate resides and simply take you directly to him.' He glared down at her and she bit her lip, knowing he had right on his side.

Thena felt shame like she had never before and tilted her head down so that her bonnet would shield the high colour in her cheeks. They burned as the guilty feelings scorched a path into her heart. Without lifting her head to meet his accusing face, she spoke quietly in her defence: 'I can explain. I promised to pay you back. I — '

'You will say and do nothing until we are in a place where prying eyes are not watching us. Then you can then tell me your whole story, and though I have no reason to and little understanding of why I am prepared to, I will listen and judge you accordingly.'

'Who are you to judge me?' she responded instantly, lifting her chin. Then she realised how foolish she was being, for he had the law on his side.

'I am a barrister, woman! You thieved from a man who has spent years studying the law of the land before he went to fight for it, and I am repaid by being the victim of a common cut-purse.'

'I am not common, nor am I a cutpurse. I think that is why you are prepared to listen to me. You know there is more to this, and to me, than that. You see it and sense it. I merely borrowed the money because the alternative was far worse, and I wanted to — I *intended* to — repay it.' She sniffed and held back the tirade of words that she wanted to pour out, realising now how dangerous this man was, or could be.

He walked her over to the side of the abbey wall, where a chestnut mare was tethered to the rail. It was then that Thena had her first clear look at Jerome's generous mouth framed by his strong jaw. His handsome features held strikingly deep, yet sad eyes. His looks were not grand in a Romanesque way, but in strength of character: a man who had seen many things, worldly yet still in his prime.

Jerome dropped her bag to the ground and placed a hand firmly on either side of her waist, gripping her through her pelisse, then lifted her bodily to place her sideways onto the saddle. She let out a gasp. The horse stood still, ignoring her squeal as she grabbed the saddle to keep her balance. Jerome said nothing, but picked up her bag and placed it on her lap. She had to hold on to it with one hand and the horse with the other. She could not wait for him to climb up behind her and hold her and the horse steady.

'Tell me, in your desperation and generosity, how much did I give to the abbey for your night's board?' he asked.

'Half a crown,' she replied in a quiet voice.

'My . . . how generous I am for one night's stay in what would have been a cold cell, no doubt!'

Thena sat with her back straight and looked at the road ahead of them, biting her bottom lip to stop herself from saying anything that would anger this man further. Mr Jerome Fender was a man of law. Could she have chosen a worse person to steal from? She stared at the sky from under the rim of her bonnet and prayed that he was truly a just man, for she needed one to dig her out of the mess her cousin had made for her.

'Where will you take me?' she asked, swallowing so hard that her mouth went quite dry. She thought of the prison cell she could be thrown into with goodness knew who — men and women together, possibly. Did they keep them separate by gender, by rank, or by crime? She had no idea what the rules of prison were, but they would surely be harsh; and she would be shown no mercy, as her crime was not one of debt but a true one of theft. She had stolen money, and a lot of it. Society would no doubt think more of her if she had used her body to earn it. A tear ran down her cheek, silently falling as Jerome answered her question.

'Miss Munro, you will come back with me to my room. There you will explain what possessed a woman trained or qualified in life enough to be a governess to steal from someone who had offered her help. For now, say nothing. The wench in the inn will presume you are my woman, and I do not care if she does. You have cost me enough. If you choose not to answer my questions, then I will not ask again. I will take you to the assizes in York myself and lay a formal charge.'

Thena turned her face to look down at him. 'You would do that to me, now that you know I was a governess?' she said quietly.

'Miss, even murderers can be gentlemen, vicars and politicians, and they still have to answer for their crimes. You broke the law, and you had no right to call it a loan when we had no agreement. Now be quiet, and be grateful that you have the opportunity to come with me.'

He swung up into the saddle behind her and she felt his body's warmth close to her. He wrapped one arm around her waist. She held on tightly to her bag as the animal moved forward. Propriety had left when she had fallen foul of the law; now she had to survive and stay out of prison. Then a thought crossed her mind: if Mr Fender was a barrister, he should be interested in seeking justice. He could possibly help her. Had she not been wronged by her cousin? Had he not sent her on a wild goose chase, no doubt hoping she would never return or recover from the shame of it? A flicker of hope kindled in her heart. It was a very small one that could easily be extinguished, but at least it was there. Mr Fender might take pity on her and seek out her cousin. The bully would not stand up to a man like this one, of that she was sure.

They did not go far before entering the stabling area of an inn. The serving woman did not look surprised when Jerome came in with Thena.

'Found her? Ah, good! Would she want food and a tub too?' Mary asked.

'No, I'm fine,' Thena said quickly. 'I've eaten, thank you.'

'Yes, she does,' Jerome said, completely ignoring her words.

The woman smiled, baring her ugly

teeth, and Thena wished she could turn around and just walk out. But she could hardly run to the abbey again, as she had rebuffed the mother superior's invitation to stay. She had made her bed and now would literally have to lie in it. The thought made her shiver as she looked up at the tall frame of Mr Jerome Fender. Would he expect her to lay with him?

He had muttered something to her, but having been lost in her own thoughts, Thena had quite frozen in time, with many emotions running through her. Jerome cupped her elbow and pushed her firmly in front of him so that she had to go up the wooden stairs first. His room was sparse, but there was a warm fire, and the tub was being filled by a boy and a girl who were running up and down the stairs with pails of warmed water.

'Won't take long, miss,' the girl said as she waited at the top for them to stand on the landing; the stairs were so narrow that no one could pass. 'We always have water on the fire for the laundry. Sally does it in the tub house out back,' she said before running back down.

# 6

Jerome and Thena stood in silence as they waited for the last two pails of hot water to be poured into the tub. A rough piece of soap was left on a tray on the floorboards, and there was a cloth for Thena to dry herself with, but no simple chemise was left for her modesty.

Jerome passed the girl and boy a coin each, which they heartily thanked him for, closing the door after them. Thena swallowed as he then turned and looked at her. 'Your bath awaits.' He gestured with his hand that she should go over to it.

It had been positioned in front of the small open fire. The logs crackled as it burned. The enamel shape of the tin bath had a higher back than front. Jerome picked up the only chair in the room and placed it back to back with the bath. Only a yard separated the chair and the tub, so even though they faced the opposite directions, it offered little privacy or comfort to Thena. Jerome then took hold of her bag and placed it on the floor in front of the chair.

'Miss Munro, my attention will be taken with that.' He pointed to her bag. 'You will strip off your attire, for it needs cleaning also, and climb into the water whilst it is still warm. Then as you wash yourself you can tell me your sorry tale — and please, do not think to embellish it with falsehoods, or this will be the last wash you will be able to have in any sense of relative privacy for some years to come. Gaols offer few creature comforts, and inmates are monitored.'

He stared at her for what seemed like an age to Thena. She faced him and he did not look away. But his words made her shiver. She had heard tales of people going into the workhouse and being treated like animals, almost dunked like sheep. But what did she know of such things? Her cousin had said some awful things to her in order to gain her agreement to set off on her perilous journey alone, her only comfort being a letter of reference and a guarantee of respectable employment at the other end of her journey. What a trusting fool she had been. Now look at her plight!

'You think I am going to strip down to my chemise here, and perform my ablutions, with you still in the room? You are mistaken, sir!' she said, her voice wavering slightly. 'You may think I am of low morals, but I am not. I am a lady!'

Jerome sighed and walked across the threadbare carpet to her. He pulled the ribbon of her bonnet, releasing it, and tossed it onto the bed. 'I do not *think* what you are going to do, for I know it. I am clean and you are not. You will correct that as I listen to your story and you show some trust in me, as I have absolutely no reason to trust you at all.' He sat on the chair, looking down, and opened her bag.

'You intend to rifle through my things?' she gasped. Yet she knew there was little she could do to resist if he insisted.

'Yes. I intend to review all the evidence before me. Now strip your clothes off and leave them in a pile, and plunge in, or I will remove more than your bonnet myself. Do not think for one moment a woman's screams or squeals in such a place as this would get anything more than curious glances up the stairs to add to the bored souls' mirth.' He stepped back and folded his arms as she took in his words.

'You are no gentleman!' she snapped, and slowly removed her pelisse.

'Good, as you are definitely not a lady,' he said, looking at her. 'Continue to remove every stitch. You smell; you have been on the road too long, and I can see in your eyes how inviting that water is. So please carry on.' He then looked back at the bag.

Thena had too much pride to accept

the situation, yet not enough courage to deny him and face the consequences. However, she realised every word he spoke was true. She stood at the opposite end of the tub. Her eyes were firmly focused on his back, lest he should turn around. As quickly as she could, she slipped out of her garments and into the welcoming water, which caressed her body as she slid under its spell. She was stiff from her many journeys. Closing her eyes, she let her head dip under the water level so that the roots of her hair could be massaged by her fingers as she cleaned it. When she sat up, trying to keep as low to the water level as possible with her knees tucked up to her naked breasts, she begun to soap herself. Then she heard Jerome speak — for one fleeting second she had started to enjoy the bath and had forgotten he was there.

'Now, Miss Parthena Munro, begin talking. I would know the exact truth — no embellishments and no untruths.'

Jerome was soon sure that her bag held few secrets. She had a letter of introduction written for her by her cousin, thanking Mr Bartholomew Squires for offering Miss Parthena Munro a place as governess to his two sons. It seemed genuine, and would have sufficed along with the reference from a Reverend Dilworth stating her good character and her family's pedigree. She was obviously well connected, yet this had not stopped her being turned out by this cousin, Mr Bertram Munro. Well, it was not an uncommon situation for a single young woman to find herself in. Parthena's future was dependent upon the goodwill of her male relations to look after her, arrange for an introduction to a prospective husband, or find her a position, such as that of governess. If what she was telling him was true, this cousin had sent a young woman, unchaperoned, to a house from which the people had apparently moved before he'd even written the letter.

Jerome began to understand how desperate she must have been. He glanced to his left as he heard her step into the tub. The looking-glass above the table in the corner of the room offered him an unexpected and very pleasant view as she gracefully entered the water; he was mesmerised. The sight of her beautiful, firm breasts stirred his deepest desires. His hand tightened on the handle of the bag as she turned her back, ready to slide down into the water. Her exquisite lean body slowly captivated his vision, the curve of her buttocks as they disappeared from view making him breathe slowly and deeply. His mind told him what he should be doing, but a very different part of his anatomy was telling him what he wanted to do.

Thena's hair was the only part of her visible — the colour of a cornfield in sunshine. Jerome stared back at the bag in front of him, closed it, and controlled his breathing and thoughts, repeating the word *thief* in his mind to dampen any desire he had for this woman. It was not only her eyes that were captivating; he now had seen more of her that took his breath away. He shook his head; a hardened soldier had returned to his country to become an incurable romantic. This would never do.

Her words began to drift over him, but she gave him a tale that was backed up by the letters he had read. Mind you, she would have to be a complete fool to tell him a tale that was at odds with them. However, even the smallest details added up, so he had no reason to disbelieve her. It all tallied with what the blacksmith and the mill man had said, as well as what she herself had said at the convent.

'Did you honestly think that you could get away with robbing a total stranger?' he asked when she finished, his voice slightly husky.

'I just did not think. I did not know

what else I could do. If I asked for charity, with all the men returned from the war, I would have been laughed at or worse. They were not going to offer me help; they would have offered me warmth for a night.'

'*I* did,' he said. 'I said nothing other than I would help you.'

'I thought you, too, were offering me something that I could not accept,' she said quietly. 'I had sunk low, but not that low.'

'What was that, then?' he asked.

'I thought you would want to give a bed for the night as payment for . . . ' She could not find the words. Aware of the water cooling, and her nakedness, she stood up and stepped out of the tub, wrapping the piece of towel around her body and dabbing herself dry by the fire.

Jerome had spied her in the looking-glass, but quickly turned his head away again. He would take no joy from her knowledge that he had seen her in the flesh, although he could think of many a way they could find joy together if she was willing.

Thena asked him to throw her clean chemise from her bag, and a dress. She watched as he produced the chemise, but was horrified when he walked over to her and handed it to her personally. 'The dress . . . you forgot it . . . I have a day dress I can change into.' She pointed to her bag. 'You must have seen it.'

'Wear that and slip under the covers of the bed and warm up properly.' He flipped back the bed cover.

'Do you intend to rape me now — is that it?' Her eyes were wide with fear, but as he stepped right up to her, with only the thin fabric between him and her body, she was feeling more than fear. He placed one finger under her chin and tilted it up so that her lips were almost touching his as he leaned down to her. She could feel his warmth, smell his musk, and sense his desire. He kissed her ever so tenderly, his lips lightly brushing hers. With the fire warming her back and him warming her heart, she was confused, but before she could turn away he suddenly stepped back and smiled at her.

'Do not flatter yourself, Miss Munro. I have business to attend to. You will stay here and await my return. To venture downstairs would be a big mistake.'

Thena glanced over her shoulder, full of shame. She blamed only herself for her recent misfortunes — well she blamed her cousin first, but her actions of late had been of her own volition. She watched as Jerome picked up her bag and headed for the door. 'You can't take that!' Fear crept up her spine at the thought that his repayment for her dishonesty might be to desert her, leaving her penniless and nearly naked in such a place. Did he seek her total ruination?

He bent down and collected the dress she had taken off as well. 'Yes, I can. I intend to for your own good.'

'But what am I to wear?' Panic

threatened to overwhelm her. Her legs trembled as tears welled up inside her.

'The chemise, I told you. Now slip into bed and do not venture outside of the room. You would definitely not get far here dressed like that. I will be back shortly.'

'Will you?' The words slipped out of her mouth as a desperate plea, and he paused. Her question hung in the air and momentarily he did not answer her. A tear trickled down her cheek.

'You will have to learn to trust me, as I did you.' He could not look her in the eye as he left.

★ ★ ★

Jerome did not intend to go far away at all. He could not risk Thena running again or being discovered. She was a soul who needed saving, but she was also desperate, and that desperation had already led her to commit an act of great folly. Fortunately it had been against him rather than any other returning soldier.

He asked the girl, Sally, if the laundry she had mentioned could clean Miss Munro's dress and undergarments. He then booked his room for a further night.

'Food for the young miss?' Mary asked as she approached him. She held forward a pewter plate onto which something resembling stewed pork and turnip had been poured. It looked warm, though not enticing; but it was sustenance after all.

'Thank you.' He took it. For a moment he stood there holding Thena's bag in one hand and the plate of food in the other. Then he shook his head and carried both back up the stairs. He had intended to teach the girl a lesson, but those beautiful eyes had moistened and, despite her brave efforts, she had cried. He could not do it. Whatever wrong she had done him, another wrong added to it did not make his actions right. Instead he returned to her, rather than letting her fear any more.

He dropped the bag to open the door. As it opened wide, Miss Munro stood with a blanket wrapped around her. He could not but admire her. She was beautiful; she would have been a total waste as a mill-worker or even as a governess.

'This is for you.' He pushed the bag inside the room with his foot and placed the plate on the small table at the side of the window. Then he dragged the tub onto the landing, where it could be seen to without them being disturbed further. Before stepping back into the room, he slipped downstairs, returning with a bottle of wine and two glasses. It was time for them to talk honestly and for him to help her.

He found her checking her bag when he returned. She had slipped her day dress on, an ice-blue muslin gown that complemented her eyes and fair hair, which hung loose over her shoulders. It was still slightly damp, but as it dried the blonde wisps only added to the ethereal impression of the faerie he had first seen in the night.

'You are quite beautiful, Miss Munro,' he said, placing the wine and glasses on the table.

'I don't know what you want of me, or to do with me,' Thena began, 'but please let us be honest with each other, as flattery will not soften the blow. Just state what terms you are offering me, if any, for the wrong I have done you to be righted. I know you could have me hanged; I am guilty, and I have no defence I can make that will stand in law.' She was holding her hands in front of her, turning one anxiously with the other as if to steady them. They were shaking, and he saw in that moment how scared she was of him; of her plight and her own stupidity. It was then Jerome knew what he wanted for them both — but how to win it without her feeling obligated or scared of him? He had never threatened a woman before, and he had no intention of starting now, but she must understand the gravity of what she had done.

'You are bold and brave as well as misguided in your judgement.' He lifted the chair over so that she could sit at the small table, then poured the wine. He took his and sat purposefully back on the bed against the headboard so he did not crowd her, and sipped, glad of the soothing taste, which he was pleasantly surprised to discover was quite mellow. Definitely French, he thought. He wondered when the inn's cellars had last been checked for contraband, for obviously that was what he was drinking. Perhaps it was liquor that was not served to the local soldiers — unless they were taking a cut as well, of course.

'You were in a dire situation, Miss Munro,' he said, looking at Thena. 'What you did was very wrong, though, as you now realise.' He watched her poke her food with the spoon.

'Yes, I do know,' she replied without looking back at him.

'Then let us look into the circumstances that forced your hand, whilst you eat. For I have no wish to have you hanged, pilloried, or even chastened for your crime. From this moment on, we shall only talk about what drove you to it, and what could make an end of your dilemma. I give you my word on it.'

Her head shot up. 'You do not intend to . . . ?' She swallowed.

'I am not a destroyer of young maids in any form of the word. I would gain little by throwing you to the wolves, who would relish having you at their mercy inside a gaol. Nor would I stoop so low as to take advantage of a young lady who has fallen on hard times. So, having established those two facts, please trust me, and tell me about this cousin of yours — but eat as well as talk, and enjoy the wine, for it is quite pleasant.'

'Thank you,' Thena replied, and smiled for the first time since they had met. Jerome saw her composure change, and the frightened wench transformed into a more relaxed, beautiful woman. Jerome had a heart to win over — hers; for as he sipped his wine, his thoughts returned to the notion of having a wife with whom he could build a future, and he was considering the possibility that fate may have brought her to him.

The warmth that swept through his body was not of the wine's making, but of the small kindling of joy that grew in his heart. A soldier's heart had returned from the wars, but a romantic's one was slowly replacing it, and he felt alive again. Jerome had no time for the words of Byron that turned maid's heads as well as those of married women who should know better. He smiled at Thena, knowing that the words he wanted to say to the right person at the correct moment were simply, 'I love you. Be my wife.' He had found what he sought; now he had to try to convince the young lady that she wanted the same.

# 7

'Parthena,' Jerome said simply, after she had finished her meal.

'Thena, please.' She looked at him. 'You have every right to call me that. If we are to be friends, then I would have you know me by the name one would call me.'

'Only if you wish it,' he said.

'Yes, I do.'

Her smile was infectious. 'Very well. Now tell me more of this Mr Bertram Munro, who sent you away.'

'Cousin Bertram had been to York three months earlier and had met up with some friends, the Park-Hamiltons. They were well connected, as Bertram had met Archibald at Cambridge and said he had bumped into him from time to time in Boodles in Pall Mall when he was in London. They were to meet me off the coach, but no one was there. I waited, but still no one came, so after an hour I made enquires and managed to find their town house.'

'I suspect Bertram already knew you were going to miss these people who were to employ you. If he had met this Archibald Park-Hamilton three months earlier, the man would surely have mentioned that in less than a month he was moving abroad.' He shook his head, distracted at the realisation that was dawning upon him. This Bertram had wanted shot of his charge, and cared not how he lost her.

'How do you know how long it was since they left . . . Jerome?' Thena asked. She tucked her hands around her knees, balancing her feet on the edge of the bed. To Jerome she looked a vision, as she was totally hooked by his words. When fear left, her persona changed, and he could feel her inner calm.

'Otherwise, whyever would he have sent you away without a chaperone, with no place or person to turn to?' He leaned forward and placed his empty glass on the table next to hers.

'Bertram had intended to come with me — or that is what he told me; but then his gout played up and he was unable to travel. Then Reverend Dilworth was kind enough to step in and offered to see me to the coach. He stayed long enough to make sure that I was seated safely and waved me off.'

'Or perhaps he just made sure you left on it,' Jerome added, deep in thought.

'But he is a good man. My father trusted Reverend Dilworth; he had been in the parish for more than fifteen years.' She turned her chair to face him.

'Who knows what tempts men,' Jerome commented without making further accusation. He needed facts.

'Can I ask you . . . did you mean what you said earlier?' she asked directly, but her cheeks flushed slightly, giving her slight embarrassment away.

'About helping you? Yes.' He swung his legs onto the floor so that he was sitting opposite her, their knees almost touching. 'I will not report you, I give you my word. Now, you must put that behind us, as I have.'

'I thank you for that and I accept your word on it. But I was referring to your comment earlier — what you meant when you said that I would be flattering myself to think that a gentleman such as you would want to touch a person such as me?'

Her confidence had grown, for she was staring directly at him; yet still he found her in a beguiling and impressionable way. She really wished to know. He took her hand in his and lightly held it. She did not pull it away.

'I wish only to know what you meant,' Thena repeated. 'I'm not offering . . . ' She tried to pull her hand out of his, but he gently held on to it.

'I meant to offend you,' Jerome said. 'It was beneath me, and it appears I have succeeded. Forgive me that one ill thought-out comment, for it was a cruel slight, and could not be further from what I actually wanted to do. Believe me, you are a beautiful lady, and one I whom suspect has been wronged morally, if not legally. I have therefore arranged for us to stay here one more night so that we may catch the York coach tomorrow. From there we will visit your cousin and see what he has to say to you when you return to him, unannounced and unharmed.' He smiled, for this would certainly prove to be an interesting distraction that would detain him from visiting his mother.

'How will I explain your presence?' Thena asked curiously.

'You will not, for I intend to call upon your cousin as a visitor, after I have collected some more facts. You will say that the family had left, as he presumably knew they had, and that you were generously provided with the ticket for the coach by your old friends at the abbey. Make no further embellishment of the story, because when the truth is to be bent, it is safer to bend it with the fewest words possible. That way, lies cannot be determined and unpicked so easily.'

He saw her lift her face and smile at him again. 'Thank you,' she said, and then asked, 'What will I do, once back in the house?'

'I suggest that you behave as if you are quite upset by the ordeal — ill, even. Take to your bed for a day to rest from your journeying and then spend time indoors out of your cousin's way, whilst I make my arrival. It should only be a day or so before I join you. If you should have access to his study whilst he is out of the house, perhaps you could delve a little into his papers and see what his letters can reveal of his plans. Do you know if your father left a will, or did your cousin inherit as he died intestate?'

'I was told that none was found, but I did not believe it to be the case as Father was always so meticulous about his business dealings. However, he would have left the estate to my cousin, or my husband if I was married, of that I am certain.' She looked away, then boldly back at him. 'He did not think that ladies were made to cope with the fine detail of business,' she added.

'Such as Boodles, no doubt.' He half-smiled. 'No matter; we have some facts to find out and digging around to do. Do not mention me, or what you did; that is between us, and it is forgotten. Now we must find out what motive this cousin of yours has for wanting you out of his way. Do you know who dealt with your father's legal affairs?' Jerome asked hopefully.

Thena shrugged her shoulders. 'He never involved me in anything like that. Even when Mother was alive, he was meticulous about keeping anything to do with his affairs away from the family. He strongly believed that ladies should not have to worry over such things,' she said, and laughed. 'The thing is, what he could never understand was that we worry more through the not knowing of such details.'

'Many men do as well, but I take your point as a very valid one. It is always the unknown that distresses people more.'

'Mr Fender . . . '

'Jerome,' he corrected.

'Very well. Jerome, why would you do all this for me?'

'Because, Thena, I believe in justice as well as enforcing the law of the land. I am an advocate for reform. Why should a person be hanged for the theft of a crust of bread to feed their starving family, the same as someone who stole ten pounds? Circumstances should be taken into account as well as the crime. And there are more people like me who are trying to change harsh laws. So, Thena, you have told me what had befallen you, and I accept the truth of it. Are we to be friends?'

'I think we already are. You are certainly being a far better friend to me than I have been to you. I shamed myself, and . . . '

He leaned forward as he stood and

gently kissed her forehead. 'That is in the past. Now let us focus on the future. We stay here one more night and leave on the morning coach. No fear is necessary; you are safe. You shall sleep under the covers and I on top. It is our business, and no one else will know. I am a practical man, that is all, and you will be safer in a room with me than in one on your own in such a place.'

Thena watched as he carried the tray outside the room and left it on the floor for the servants to collect. Returning to her, he stared out of the small window that overlooked the stable yard. 'I have a horse to see to. Would you care to join me? We can explore the town of Gorebeck, and perhaps find you a new pair of boots. You have all but destroyed those on your cross-moor adventure.'

She looked down at her feet. They were a sorry sight, even though the nuns had tried to resurrect her boots, especially when seen next to the finer quality of her dress. 'I owe you so much already, Jerome,' she said.

'Perhaps, but it is of no consequence. Fate has brought us together, Thena, so let us not fight that and instead work together to unravel the knot of deception that I suspect your cousin has formed. Do not forget, I am a man of law. I shall unravel his knots and see that you have what is yours by right. If anyone needs bringing to justice, I think it will be him.'

'But have you nothing else you should be doing? Are you not a busy man? You gain nothing from all of this?' Thena asked, and saw a slow smile cross his handsome face.

'I was busy at war, but no longer. I should be returning to my dear mama, who will be wanting to see me settled down in a legal practice with a society wife, positioned in a respectable home. So you are quite wrong, for I believe I have much to gain by doing the correct thing by you.'

Thena stood and pulled on her pelisse. 'Then I have been fortunate indeed.'

# 8

Thena stood before the old grit-stone Jacobean building. Leaham Hall had been in her family for two generations and had been her father's pride and joy. His grandfather had saved the life of a lord, and in his gratitude that lord had left one of his estates to him along with a legacy that would be able to keep it going.

The legacy — what had happened to it? And why had she been so easily cast off? Her father's greatest sorrow had been his inability to beget a son and heir, but he had always been a loving, caring father to her and never begrudged her anything. Thena did not consider for one moment the possibility that he would not look to her future also. He knew that his heart was weakening and had had time to prepare, so why would he not leave a will?

She swallowed back unshed tears, for this was her home no more, and now she had to face the man — a stranger to her — who had planned her fall. Her anger stopped her from giving in to melancholy. Instead she raised her head high as she walked up to the door of the building that should have been the entrance to her home, and paused. Should she knock, or enter? Then she smiled. She would be damned if she was going to knock on her own door. She turned the large iron handle and swung the door open wide before walking boldly in, dropping her bag on the floor inside the hallway.

Elsie Hubbart, the upper house maid, was the first person Thena saw as she scuttled from the servants' stairs toward the day room.

'Mrs Hubbart!' Thena snapped. She had not intended to give the woman a fright, but if she had seen a ghost the effect upon her could not have been less dramatic.

'Miss Munro!' The woman almost

ran to her. 'It is so good to see you here, miss, but I was not expecting you.' She took Thena's pelisse off her as she spoke. 'Are you on your own? Is Reverend Dilworth with you?' She looked around, staring down the gardens to the ornate iron gates that marked the entrance to the property and separated it from the village beyond. The drive led to the main road and the market square of the small village of Leaham. It was a fairly secluded place, and pretty as a picture in Thena's eyes. Unlike the harsher reality of the market town she had just left, this place was like a haven, unspoilt and simple.

'No, he is not.' Thena was not about to begin explaining events to a servant. 'Take my bag to my room. I hope my trunk has not been sent on already. It was supposed to be forwarded when I wrote to my cousin, letting him know that all was well and I had arrived safely.'

Thena now realised that he was most

likely going to keep what small treasures she had of her life here, as that letter would never arrive. Instead it would tell of a desperate woman who had resorted to God knew what existence in order to survive. Once fallen, in any respect, he could cast her off, and no one would want to know her ... well, none of their previous acquaintances.

She shook her head. If she had not seen those poor people returning from war with no work to go to, or the lame, or the poor souls who toiled at the mills, would she have given them a second thought? Or, more likely, she would have grouped them together as the poor, wretched and ignorant without considering why they lived as they did. Her brief scrape with life as a felon had changed her. From happy, protected Parthena, she had had her eyes opened; and as she thought of her new friend, Jerome, her heart welled with gratitude, admiration and desire. He had seen her as a thief, judged her, and found her a worthy person. He knew her for what she was, and yet he had still helped her.

Mrs Hubbart broke through her thoughts. 'Miss, we heard no word from you. The trunk has been stored in the attic room, I believe.' She looked quite ashen-faced.

'You believe?' Thena said.

'Yes, miss, although Mr Munro was talking of having it brought down again this weekend.'

'Where is Mr Bertram now?' Thena could not smell the smoke from his pipe hanging in the air, and so guessed he was either out or still abed.

'He is out, miss, but should be back by noon. He has been busy preparing the Hall, miss,' she added.

Thena suspected that Mrs Hubbart wanted to share something with her. 'Preparing the Hall for what?' she asked.

'We have been told that at the end of the month it is to go on the market for sale, miss.'

Thena stared at her, not knowing quite what to say. Her home was to be sold, without her knowledge. She stared at the servant who had served her father well for years and felt sad for her also. 'What is to become of you and the staff?' she asked. This question would never have crossed her mind before her recent excursion.

'We have been told to hope the next owner keeps us on, and if not, Mr Munro says we can always look for work in the village. But there *is* no work in the village, and no one wants to leave to go to them mills, miss. So we all hope that we will be taken on. Perhaps you could speak to the master on our behalf and ask if we could be part of the arrangements?' she asked tentatively.

Thena recognised the tinge of desperation in Mrs Hubbart's voice and understood it. 'I will speak to him about his plans when he has returned from his business, and we'll see. Now, please make my room ready. Warm it through and have my trunk brought back down to it. Why it should have been placed in the attic, I have no notion. I would have my clothes back where they belong. Be assured, Mrs Hubbart, that I will speak to my cousin. Let me know as soon as he returns. I would like to surprise him.' She forced a smile.

'Thank you, Miss Munro . . . Miss, are you feeling well?'

'Whyever do you ask?' Thena was puzzled by expression upon the maid's face.

'Sorry, miss; you just seem different in some way.' Thena was shaking herself out of her thoughts as Mrs Hubbart smiled and quickly added, 'Well everything changes in time.' She shrugged her shoulders, and Thena watched her run up the stairs as quickly as her feet would allow.

Breathing out slowly, Thena walked into the library, remembering times spent with her father fondly, and then looked to the adjacent door of his study. If Bertram was not to return till noon, there was an hour clear. She entered through the large doorway and stared at the polished walnut desk. It had papers scattered all over it. Her father would turn in his grave at the mess. He had always left everything orderly — always. That was why it was so difficult for Thena to believe he had not left a will.

She glanced out of the window to see if there was any sign of Bertram returning, but there was not. Curiously rather than guiltily, she opened a large folder on his desk and read the documents that were to hand, glancing quickly over accounts, bills and tenancies. Looking at the plans that had been drawn, she began to understand the gravity of the scheme Bertram was set on. It seemed he was planning to sell off everything. There was a drawing of the river with the buildings redrawn. It was then that she realised these new buildings were of a mill and crammed-in accommodation for workers. Bertram was planning to destroy the Hall and the farms, and consequently the whole village would change.

Another drawing outlined the row of slightly grander terraced housing that would face the village square. The dwellings would not fit in with the natural scheme of things at all. It was a lot to take in. If Bertram had his way, this village that had survived the plague and gone on to prosper for centuries was about to become another mill town; there would be nothing peaceful left about it. The house staff would find work, but it would be in a noisy, dusty factory. Thena resolved to tell Jerome and stop this. How this was to be accomplished, she did not know — but what of the legacy that went with the land? Perhaps it would have some clause within it that could be used. She put the papers and drawings back as she found them.

She knew that she needed to leave, but in desperation she looked through the desk drawers. She found no further information concerning the will or the estate, but now she knew at least why Bertram wanted free rein to do as he pleased. He had big plans, but she had a weapon that he knew nothing about: Mr Jerome Fender.

With that surprisingly pleasant thought, she quickly made her way up to her old room. It was still very much as she had left it. Mrs Hubbart had lit the fire. Thena could almost believe that time had gone back and her home was hers once more. Her father had said to her on one occasion, as they stood before the grandfather clock in the hallway, that time could be a good friend or a heavy enemy, depending on how you used it. The clock hadn't worked for years, but he had told her he used time well, for it was his friend. She loved his fanciful side; but like the clock, his life had stopped too soon.

Thena prepared to welcome her cousin. He was about to learn that it was not so easy to rid himself of her. Then she had another thought. If her father had left a will and her cousin had hidden or destroyed it, then perhaps it stood in the way of what he had planned for the estate. In which case, they had a lot to prove, in very little time.

★　★　★

Jerome arrived in the village of Leaham after following the chaise to the estate, knowing that Thena should have arrived safely at the Hall. He first walked toward the picturesque village square, in the centre of which was a small water fountain. There he allowed his horse to drink while he lifted his small bag off the saddle and surveyed the buildings around him. In particular, he noted the presence of legal offices, an inn, a small hotel and coffee house, a milliner, saddler and blacksmith. The small apothecary and dispensary was next to a grocer's shop.

The offices of Messrs. Blackmore, Hide and Stanton, legal representatives, were next to Farthings and Crutch

Undertakers. Jerome noted the name Stanton. It was common enough, but he had studied with a Geoffrey Stanton and taken exams at the same time as him . . . Fate, he mused, could be a wonderful thing if it was working in your favour.

He was about to enter the inn when a coach drew up in front of it. The man who alighted made straight for the coffee house. Letting his intuition guide him, Jerome did likewise. It was then he saw a familiar face seated at a table with a rotund-looking man. Both had greeted the gentleman from the coach but had not seen Jerome enter behind him. Fascinated, Jerome slipped surreptitiously into a bay, determined to make himself comfortable behind the table where the group had gathered.

'Charles, good man, glad you could make it. Please sit down, sir. You know Stanton here. How was your journey?' The man's voice almost fawned.

'Not too bad, Bertram. So tell me, who is this person?' The newly arrived gentleman's confident drawl was patronising, and Jerome disliked him straight away. He smiled to himself: he was indeed suited to be a judge, as in his time watching people in court on both sides of the bench he had gained an insight into a person's character by listening to what they did or did not say.

Drinks were ordered, and Jerome could not hear much more of their initial small talk as he, too, was served by a friendly young woman.

'No,' Bertram's voice rose; then, as if remembering where he was, he lowered it and continued, 'I tell you, she took herself off to North Yorkshire on the whim of becoming a governess. She ranted about making use of her education. I tell you, I have never heard such nonsense coming out of the mouth of a young lady. She was indulged as a child, for why else should a girl become such a wilful creature? It is not a quality that endears a person. I have not heard a word from her since.

It is a bad business, Stanton.'

'So where does this leave things, Bertram?' Charles asked. 'Whatever the rash act of this girl was, it is of no consequence to our agreement, is it?'

'Well, as I understand it, the legacy only attaches itself to the direct line, and blocks an heir from selling the estate. If there is no son or no son-in-law to inherit, the land and all that is on and under it passes in its entirety to the next of kin, however distant they may be.' Bertram cleared his throat. 'Is that not correct, Stanton?'

'Yes, it seems so,' Geoffrey Stanton replied. 'Perhaps it was not intended for the legacy to be so limiting in its terms, but the devil is in the wording, and we must follow them to the letter. However, this lady appears to have acted in haste. She is naïve, and I am sure cannot have travelled far.'

Geoffrey Stanton was being very considerate of Thena, Jerome realised. Perhaps the man did not believe all that Bertram was saying. Jerome hoped so, for he could be a useful ally for Thena.

'I agree,' Bertram said, shaking his head in pretend-exasperation. 'If she had stayed, right now I could be finding her a suitor. But the headstrong, foolish girl ran away, and I cannot trace her whereabouts; it would be impossible unless I found a farmhand with as tarnished a reputation as hers. Still, that will never happen, as an estate needs a gentleman to run it effectively, not a simple-minded girl or a labourer,' he scoffed. 'The address she gave me was false, and no one seems to have any knowledge of where she is. Who, of any breeding, would even look twice at her now?' He sighed.

Geoffrey spoke, and Jerome was now convinced that he was definitely his fellow ex-student. 'I am most bemused that she has been so bold,' he said. 'However, until we can locate Miss Munro, should we not delay the sale of the estate, lest there be any challenge made? After all, is it not possible she may have eloped?'

'What?' Bertram exclaimed. 'Preposterous! There is no suitor. And besides, the girl's father never bothered her with the details of the will. Why would he? So what challenge could she make? It is highly unlikely that she will announce an engagement under the circumstances. No, I am afraid Miss Parthena Munro has thrown her last tantrum. The paperwork is explicit, and Charles has other options to consider. We must move forward with this. Likewise, I have wasted enough time here. I need to return to Kent. Mother will be most anxious that things are sorted out, and quickly.'

'Indeed,' Charles agreed. 'The girl is irrelevant. Bertram has inherited the estate, and we have an agreement. Now I expect the paperwork to be finalised by the end of this month. If it is too big a job for you, Stanton, then I will consult my London lawyers . . . ' He allowed his voice to trail off.

'I think our business is done here.' Geoffrey Stanton pushed back his chair, scraping it on the floor. 'I will see to the paperwork and will be in touch. Mr Munro, Mr Tripp, I bid you good day. I, too, have much to do.'

Jerome watched Geoffrey leave, and smiled. Good — they had upset him. He would not like the jibe about him being inferior to the London lawyers. Geoffrey had fought prejudice all through his studies, as his father had made his money through trade. This meant that Bertram and his nefarious colleague Charles might have lost his loyalty. If Jerome went to him now, with care, things could well play into his hands. Bertram had obviously not seen Thena yet, but he was busy painting a very different image of her than Jerome knew to be true.

He turned his glass around on the table. What they did next had to be carefully thought out. Bertram was hiding the truth from Thena, and he had carefully orchestrated a situation where there was only her word against his. Had she left without his blessing?

The letter she had of introduction to the family, the one Jerome had read as she bathed, said that she had been sent by Bertram, but that was the only proof she had that he had arranged for her position.

Jerome was about to stand up and follow Stanton when he heard Bertram's voice rise again. 'It concerns me that my man could not confirm what happened to her. I expected a report that would give us surety that the girl will be no more trouble to us. Despite her having no other means to survive that are, shall we say, reputable, she managed to completely disappear, Charles. I tell you, this has been an ill thought-out affair. We should have been bolder.'

'Bertram, good fortune has smiled on you here; do not cast a shadow over it by tainting it with the blood of an innocent. I will not be party to that.'

'But you said to send her away and be done with her,' Bertram snapped.

'I might have made an offhand

comment. You could have sent her to a convent, had her sent overseas to have her education finished, anything. How you chose to interpret my words was down to you, and the consequences will be yours to face if she emerges as an embarrassment to either of us.'

'But . . . '

Charles sighed as Bertram protested. 'Listen, man. She will have found a way to survive, as we all must. You focus on moving the sale through. I will give you another month, and then I expect to be able to bring in my men and start work on this backwater to make it pay handsomely.' Charles sounded as if he was drawing the conversation to a close. Jerome heard his chair move back.

'Yes, yes, of course,' Bertram said. 'I was just thinking aloud. Everything will be ready. Do you wish to stay at the Hall tonight?'

'No, I have other business partners to see. I will meet you back here in four weeks to the hour and the day. Have everything ready for me, or I will buy

117

land elsewhere. Progress stops for no man, Bertram!'

'Of course. I fully understand,' Bertram grovelled as Charles returned to his coach.

Jerome watched as the vehicle drew away and Bertram cursed his so-called business partner. He then headed off in the direction of Leaham Hall, and Jerome almost wished he could be there to see his face when he arrived. However, he had to re-acquaint himself quickly with an old colleague. Glad that he had never taunted Geoffrey about his family's new money, Jerome stood and walked purposefully over to the offices of Messrs. Blackmore, Hide and Stanton.

They had some catching up to do, rather quickly, with the opportunity to help each other at the same time. Fate, Jerome again pondered, was indeed a lovely thing. He knocked on the highly polished black door and waited to be announced.

He knew that things were definitely

on an upward turn when he entered the immaculate office and Mr Geoffrey Stanton stood up to greet him with one kindly word: 'Welcome!'

# 9

'I am so pleased that you remember me, sir,' Jerome said with a bow. 'If you recall, we were in the Inns at the same time.'

Geoffrey shook Jerome's hand, looking genuinely pleased to see him. Then he took Jerome's hat and placed it carefully on a stand and closed the door to the office. 'I never forget the face of a friend. You were always a gentleman, Mr Fender — Jerome, wasn't it?'

'Yes,' Jerome replied, slightly embarrassed that he had obviously made a stronger impression on Mr Stanton than Stanton had on him.

'I know I am right, sir. I pride myself on my memory of faces and names.' He smiled.

Jerome nodded. 'An excellent memory, sir, and one that will serve you in good stead in our profession.'

'Oh, well, I'll be honest with you. I have every reason to remember you, since you stopped Giles Baglan from giving me a kicking. I admired you from that moment onwards and have followed your career with interest. Now that the war is over, we can pursue our chosen paths once more. I served in the 95th, sir. Only a lieutenant, but I did my part.' He held his head high as if he had proved himself able to fight and defend not only himself but his country.

Jerome was momentarily speechless, as he had forgotten that he did give Baglan a kicking himself for picking on the new boy. However, Jerome could well understand the impact his intervention had had on the younger Geoffrey's life. Jerome smiled even more broadly — 'one good deed' was the phrase that came to mind. They exchanged ranks and anecdotes for a few moments with enthusiasm, and then there was a slight pause in the conversation.

Stanton took his seat again after

offering Jerome a glass of sherry from his cabinet. 'So tell me,' he said, 'what brings a London barrister all the way to this backwater?'

'Justice, Geoffrey, or lack of it, is why I am here. I am an advocate for reform who thinks that the punishment should be more fitting to the crime. But first, tell me — are you unhappy here?' Jerome saw the pensive look on his colleague's face turn to curiosity.

'I, too, am for reform, but these things take time, especially where laws are concerned — as well you know. No, I am not happy at this precise moment. To be honest, I have not been for some months. I have a wife who expects our first child this coming summer, and we have been very happy in this beautiful village until relatively recently. She is a teacher, and we have such plans for it.' He then looked down at the papers upon his desk with little enthusiasm.

'Then what has changed?' Jerome asked.

'Nothing as yet, but I fear it will soon

enough. A major property on the edge of town is to be sold — an estate that holds the deeds for farms and town properties alike; and this lovely village, I feel, will not be valued by its new owner. But you catch me at a sensitive time, and I really should not be discussing such business with you, as it breaks every rule of confidentiality that we value and uphold. However . . . ' He looked up at Jerome and smiled brightly. 'As you were listing so attentively to my conversation in the coffee house, I presume that you have some interest in the affair.' He raised one eyebrow.

'Ah, Geoffrey, I am glad to see that your mind is as razor-sharp as always, and that you miss nothing. You will clearly have seen me when you returned here and glanced back, and I would add that your assumption is quite correct. The young lady you were discussing, Miss Munro, did not run away; nor is she reckless, or damaged in reputation or body in any way. She is safely returned to the home that has been hers to live in since her birth. However, I fear that she has been kept away from the truth of her father's will and the details of her inheritance, as in so doing her cousin seeks to rid himself of her and take the land. Why this man, Charles Tripp, is so interested in it, I do not know.'

'Nor I, for sure; but I have made enquiries about Mr Charles Tripp and discovered that wherever he buys — property or land — he leaves a factory where houses once stood, resulting in the destruction of the original small town or village. He has done this twice that I know of. He buys, then provides the money, plans and men to do his work, and moves on to live in his own country idyll, where he begins planning for his next victim. It is all legal, and all sickening if you are living in the path of his 'progress'. I do not care for him, or his London lawyers of whom he boasts so much. I apologise if I sound embittered, but there you have it. I do not want to live in London, and have not the money to make a name for myself there even if I did have that ambition. So how can I help you?'

'Is Parthena able, in any way, to block Bertram Munro from getting his hands on the estate?'

'Has she not shown you a copy of her father's will?' Geoffrey asked, and Jerome thought again about how evilly this impressionable, innocent young woman was being duped.

'She has not seen the will, and has in fact been told that her father died intestate,' Jerome answered, trying to conceal his anger.

'That is a lie! I left a copy for her with Bertram. I have been unable to speak to her. He insists, as her father used to, that business is for the men in the world and that she should be protected from it.'

'But not from the consequences of the men's actions, apparently.'

'That is true. The only way she can have any ownership of the land in any sense is if she is married by the end of the month, which is impossible. Then she, or rather her husband, can make a direct claim to the total inheritance. But if she had been told the truth when the will was disclosed to Bertram, they would have had six months for her to possibly find a suitor. The one thing that was personally gifted to her, along with an allowance of three hundred pounds per annum so long as the estate exists, is the grandfather clock from the hallway — and this,' he said as he leaned into his drawer and pulled out an envelope. 'This is part of the arrangements that are not mentioned in the will itself, and Mr Bertram Munro does not know about it. You see, it is a letter and key, which were entrusted to me to give to Miss Munro in the event of her twenty-first birthday, if she was not wed and he, Mr Munro senior, died before that date.'

'Do you know what it is for, and when will she be twenty-one?' Jerome asked.

'No, but she will, I am sure. She was twenty-one last Wednesday, two days after she disappeared.'

Jerome sat forward. 'Then you must give these items to her, without Bertram's presence or knowledge.'

'I agree; but you forget she is no longer here, and that presents me with a problem and a dilemma. When, if ever, do I tell her cousin about it?' He raised both hands in despair.

'You do not need to worry, for I bring good tidings. She is safely restored to her home. Mr Bertram Munro lied: she did not run away; nor is she given to fits and tantrums. Let me explain what happened, and then we will find a way for you to see her so that you can deliver that envelope to her in person. Perhaps if you could call on her tomorrow at ten? I will make sure she is at home and that Mr Bertram Munro is not.' Jerome was enraged, though he had met many an unscrupulous or greedy man who thought little of the consequences of his actions on the dependant female in his charge.

'How and why would you do this?' Geoffrey Stanton stared at him, intrigued, but he was no man's fool, so Jerome decided honesty was the best policy.

'Because I believe in justice — and because I have quite fallen under Miss Munro's spell. I would see how desperate or daring she actually is to save her estate, and the village, not to mention her future, from the likes of Mr Bertram Munro and Mr Charles Tripp.'

'Then you have my blessing, and I will do what I can to aid you. But Tripp is a very powerful man, and he could destroy me as well, Jerome. I have a family to think about.'

'You need not fear. I will not see you harmed in any way. If all goes according to my plan, we can look to a happier future. If Miss Munro turns down my offer, then I will find you a position in my own firm. You would lose a village, but gain a career. Not perhaps what you wish, but it would secure a future for that growing family of yours.' Jerome stood.

'Very well.' Geoffrey stood also, and shook his hand. 'You are a guardian angel to waifs and strays.' He smiled.

'No, Geoffrey; to a few wronged individuals.' Jerome shut off the memories of men's death screams from his recent past — battlefield blood and gore — and cleared his throat. 'Believe me, I am no one's guardian angel!' He left, trying to bury the demons deep, and focus upon his faerie of the night and his current mission to save a village from destruction.

\* \* \*

Mr Bertram Munro burst into Leaham Hall, to be greeted by Mrs Hubbart as she was about to take a warm drink of milk and honey up the stairs to Thena.

'What is the meaning of this, Mrs Hubbart? Where are you going with that? Your place is not to be seen on the main stairs!' He barked his words out before she had the chance to say anything.

'I was taking it, this drink . . . ' She held the tray up as if it was obvious. ' . . . upstairs, sir, for the young mistress.' She added, 'Who returned to us today.'

'Who returned? What nonsense do you speak, woman?' He threw his coat down on the table and tossed his hat also, but both he and Mrs Hubbart watched as it rolled across the table top and fell on the floor.

'Mrs Hubbart!' he barked. 'Pick that up!' The woman's hand began to shake as she held on to the tray, conscious that the warmed milk was beginning to spill; but she seemed more distressed by it being spoilt, and was focused upon stilling it. Her lips parted as if she was going to be bold enough to speak out, but she was interrupted and saved from the impact of a vexed retort.

'Cousin, I am so glad that you have returned. I have so much to tell you,'

Thena's voice drifted down from the upper landing.

'Parthena, is that really you?' He stood gazing up as if his world had turned.

'Yes, cousin, who else would it be?' she said as she came down the stairs.

'You . . . you are here?' He took a step backwards as if he had seen an apparition take shape in front of him. She walked calmly down the last few steps so that she stood before him.

'Well, where else would I go when I find myself unable to make the introduction you had arranged for me?' she laughed.

'But you left intent on making a new life . . . ' He was glancing awkwardly around at Mrs Hubbart.

'Of course, with your letter in my bag. But you see, the people had moved on: there was no Major Harrington, wife or sons at the address I was given. I discovered they had moved to Harrogate six months previously. So, I am afraid it was a wasted trip.' She now stood on the bottom step, staring straight at him.

He fought to regain his composure. 'But that is abominable! You must tell me what awful plight, my dear cousin, has befallen you. We must act quickly to repair your reputation and find somewhere peaceful where you can recover. How have you returned to us so . . . safely? I mean,' he carried on, 'under the circumstances, the thought of what you have been through does not bear consideration.' He was rubbing his forehead with his kerchief.

He seemed confused, and was trying to make Mrs Hubbart — who was watching — believe that Thena's reputation had been compromised by her ordeal. Well, she was not going to let him. 'Why, nothing has befallen me, Bertram!' she said, her voice deliberately patronising. 'Whatever are you thinking? My schooling was partially completed at a convent school in the town,' she said, and remembered what Jerome had taught her: that to weave a convincing lie, you merely embellished the truth on which it hung. 'I merely asked the mother superior at the abbey for help, and she gladly arranged my safe return. I was never in any peril, Bertram. Why, that would have been devastating, and I know you only had my best intentions at heart. No, I could not have been better looked after if it had all been planned that way. So you must tell me how things fare here. I understand there are to be changes made.' She glanced around at Mrs Hubbart, who was looking from one cousin to the other, taking it all in.

'We will not chatter in the hall like servants, Parthena. Come into the morning room and we shall discuss this matter further. This venture of yours may have had some grave implications,' Bertram said, keeping to his chosen theme. Then he turned to Mrs Hubbart. 'Not a word of this to anyone, Mrs Hubbart, you hear?'

'No, sir,' she said, as she made her way down the corridor and back to the servants' domain.

Thena walked ahead of Bertram. She heard him bark another order out for them not to be disturbed. He did not understand how a servant could be loyal, because he did not comprehend the meaning of the word. Thena did not like the word 'hate', with all its connotations, but the emotion she felt towards the insufferable man who had gained his position through her father's death could only be described as such. She felt no shame for feeling it, either, as he had lowered her situation to one where she had turned in a moment of weakness to theft.

Calmly Thena sat in the window seat and looked over to the marble-framed fireplace. A memory of it adorned with leaves for the Christmas season made her swallow back her nostalgia for a world and a time she could never recapture. Even if this home, by some miracle, became hers again, it would have to be updated. She would not live in a mausoleum dedicated to the past.

Bertram took his position before the fire even though it was not lit. He held his hands behind his back as if it was still giving out warmth. His girth, she noticed, seemed to be growing as the weeks passed by.

'You have been on a pointless, yet perilous, journey of folly,' he said. 'Are you certain you escaped it . . . unharmed?' He watched closely for her reaction.

She smiled back at him, innocence personified. 'I do not know what you mean, Cousin Bertram. Why would the nuns hurt me in any way? In fact, it was a joy to see the place again. I loved the abbey school, and it had not changed much at all.' She straightened her skirts as she spoke. She hated lying, but as she had decided she hated the man even more, she did it with great ease on this occasion. 'It gave me time to think about things here, and how we may have got off on the wrong footing. But as you are no doubt aware, I was grieving deeply for my poor father. I really do not know what possessed me to think of taking such a position. Of course, I should stay here and help you. After all, some of the tenants have been with the farms for generations, and I should introduce you to them.' She saw him pale.

'You took it, Parthena, because there are few options for you to consider, and staying here is not one of them. I assure you that — '

Loud knocking at the door interrupted his words.

'Damnation! Who the hell can that be? If it's a tradesman, I'll have his skin for coming to the front door. Your father was too soft with these people. They show no respect!' He stormed out of the room, muttering under his breath. Foul words under bad breath, Thena mused.

Before Mrs Hubbart could answer it, Bertram was at the door. He had dispensed with the services of her father's butler, Mr Kendal, as soon as he had been summoned to the estate.

He was a man who trusted no one and who was almost paranoid about people getting close to him or his business affairs.

Bertram flung the door open wide and was ready to blast the unsuspecting figure whom he found at the other side of it with his outrage, when he saw that standing innocently on his doorstep was a well-dressed gentleman, whose athletic frame, accentuated by his high hat and fashionably cut coat, told of money and position. This was obviously not a vision Bertram had expected to see.

'Yes? Good day, sir?' Bertram tried to regain his composure.

Jerome looked at the portly figure in front of him. 'Is the master of the house in? I would like to call upon him,' he said.

Bertram was at the point of bursting. Could he be undermined any further by women or circumstance? he seemed to be wondering. Jerome almost smiled as the man's chest filled with air at the indignation that he had been taken for the butler.

'I am he, the owner of this grand estate!' Bertram snapped.

In that moment, Jerome knew he had completely wrong-footed the man. This was going to be a meeting he would enjoy.

# 10

'My greatest apologies, sir,' Jerome said, removing his hat and allowing his dark hair to rest freely upon the collar of his coat. He removed his hand from his pocket and offered Bertram his card.

Bertram took it as he regained his composure and stared at the man's address in The Inns of Court, London. 'My dear sir, to what do I owe this pleasure? Please, come in.' He stepped back and shouted, 'Mrs Hubbart!'

The woman appeared from the servants' corridor. 'Yes, Mr Munro?' She stopped and looked at Jerome. 'Oh, another visitor! I mean, let me take your coat, sir.' She busied herself around Jerome.

'Arrange for a tray to be sent to my study,' Bertram ordered her, then turned back to Jerome. 'Now, do tell me to what I owe this visit, sir.'

'I bumped into an old friend of mine, Mr Charles Tripp,' Jerome began. 'I believe you and he are well acquainted, and he suggested that I call. Is this a good time?' He let his voice tail off as Bertram walked ahead towards a door that was presumably the study. However, Jerome stopped and stepped back when he spied Thena in the doorway opposite. He looked at her and winked. She was even more beautiful when dressed in her normal finery; those beautiful eyes looked pleased to see him. Her manner was relaxed in her natural surroundings.

She quickly walked over to him as she had that first night. It was only a few days ago, yet in that short period of time she had worked her magic upon him. How much he knew of her: her body, her secrets and her plight . . . and how much more he would love to know.

If his mother had introduced him to a daughter of one of her society friends, the dating ritual would have played itself out, and they would be wed after months of polite visitations; yet they still might be as strangers on their wedding night. Before the wars, Jerome would have been happy with that; but not now. He valued life, passion and hope and cared not for trinkets and trivia. With Thena he would know the real woman, the true self that normally hid behind a veneer. A woman strong enough in mind and body to do what was needed to survive. She had ventured across the open moor trods on her own! There was a woman who stood at one with nature, and he was even surer now that she was the woman whom he sought: his life partner and soulmate.

But first, to sort out this mess. Bertram was saying something to him as he walked on, lost in his thoughts and presuming Jerome would follow him. Jerome quickly mouthed to Thena as he passed her: 'Be here at eleven o'clock tomorrow morning. You will have a visitor.'

Bertram turned and saw Jerome looking back. He realised who must have caught his attention and moved to stand between them, clearing his throat. 'Please let me introduce you to my ward and cousin, Miss Parthena Munro.' He looked at her as if she was a naughty, intrusive child.

'I am pleased to meet you, miss.' Jerome saw her eyes glint with humour.

'This gentleman has come to talk to me from his offices in London, on business. We will finish our discussion later, Parthena. Now do run along, my dear,' Bertram instructed her. Jerome saw a distinct flash of anger cross her eyes, but he raised an eyebrow and she took the hint.

'Of course, cousin,' she said. 'Until later, Bertram, and Mr . . . ?' She looked innocently at Jerome.

'Mr Jerome Fender at your service, miss,' he said, and bowed slightly. He saw the faintest hint of a smile on those lovely sensuous lips, and decided that the two of them had played this scene out long enough. He looked at Bertram and gestured toward the study. 'Shall we?'

'Of course,' Bertram said, and led him into the room, closing the door tightly. The brief discussion of the weather and the state of the older roads ended once a tray was in place and Mrs Hubbart had, like Thena, disappeared from their presence.

'So, please tell me why Charles has requested that you visit me,' Bertram began. 'Is this in connection with Stanton and our business dealings?'

Jerome crossed his legs and leaned back casually in the fireside chair. Bertram was resting against his desk; Jerome did not want to sit opposite him and give him the opportunity to feel he was superior, or in control of the situation. For his plan to work, Jerome needed two things to happen: firstly, to convince this worm of a man that he was stubbornly in earnest regarding the 'business' of which he intended to speak; and secondly, that Thena's willingness to solve this problem and save her village was as strong as his desire to have her as his wife. For it never occurred to him that she would want him after the way they had met. He had seen her brought low, and knew she was a woman who had pride as well as beauty.

'I am of the understanding that you and Charles are soon to complete a deal for this Hall,' Jerome said, 'and that by the end of the month all must be arranged and the deeds handed over.'

'Yes, we are,' Bertram confirmed. 'But, sir, if you wish to bid for the Hall yourself, I must inform you that the land attached to this estate includes many farms and shops, forestry and also the river rights. There is a tin mine and unmined seams of copper. So, in all, you would need a large sum to outbid Charles.' He flashed an avaricious smile. 'However, I am a fair man, and Charles understands that there is no room for sentiment in business.' He shrugged his shoulders, as if dismissing any notion that his words were disloyal or underhand. His eyes were fixed on Jerome as he waited for his reaction.

'Indeed, which is precisely why I am not making a bid for the estate,' Jerome replied. He did wish, however, that he had enough reserves separate from the family estate to actually buy everything; for here he had seen a peaceful, functioning community that had even more potential if the people could be allowed to look after their land themselves. In order to gain access to Thena and explain his rather outlandish plan, Jerome had to have Bertram on side. He recalled what Bertram had told Charles after Geoffrey had left the coffee house; there was no mistaking how callously this man would behave to get what he desired. However, if he suspected that Jerome had Thena's interests at heart — or God forbid, the desire to wed her, which would give him the inheritance — he would never agree to anything Jerome proposed. Jerome must therefore persuade this pitiful excuse of a man that he was in the pay of Charles in some way, and would willingly remove Thena from their path, temporarily or permanently.

'No, it is not the land I want, sir,' Jerome continued, 'as my Kent estate takes up so much of my time when I am not in Pall Mall.' He saw Bertram's eyes light up. 'It is the young lady who interests me, especially after setting eyes upon her again just now in all her beauty. I understood from Charles that she had vanished from your care; and yet I realised, when I met him at The Turnpike Inn to discuss our other business, that the lady I had seen alight from the coach and asking for transport to Leaham Hall was in fact your missing cousin.'

'I do not follow.' Bertram was becoming agitated. 'What would Charles be discussing Miss Munro with you for, sir? I assure you, if you are considering a rushed engagement or some sort of land grab, then I have to tell you that as her legal guardian — '

His words were interrupted when Jerome burst forth with laughter. He calmed himself and coughed. 'My very good man! How lowly you think of me and my reputation. Despite the fact that I would be breaking the law of bigamy, as my own dear wife would hardly agree to move over to make room for the girl, the idea that I would risk my career on hitching myself to a wayward creature is very amusing.' He shook his head. 'Indeed, I do not doubt she has some good breeding, but you are talking about a wench who will up and run away at the first sign of things not going her way. No, that is not what I meant at all.' He shook his head to stress his disbelief.

'Oh, forgive me. I misunderstood.' Bertram looked greatly relieved, but was quite flustered or excited by the turn of events.

'I have the ability to remove her and lose her for you, quite legitimately, without question, if that would help,' Jerome said, and leaned forward, interlacing the fingers of his hands in front of him as he did so. 'Are you interested? For although I would gain entertainment from this distraction, I will not stay and repeat my offer. I have a reputation to uphold.'

'But how would you do this, and why?' Bertram was now sitting on the edge of the chair he had pulled up opposite Jerome, leaning and listening with intensity to his visitor's words.

Jerome deliberately leered at him. He had this blackguard in the palm of his hand. Cousin Bertram was blinded by greed and not blessed with the greatest intelligence, common sense, or conscience, it seemed. 'Very simply, for a debt owed to a dear friend who, when your deal is secured, will see me right anyway,' he said.

'Very well. How will you do this?' Bertram whispered.

'I mean to invite her to London to be a companion to my dear young sister Eleanor for the season, and offer her the delights and fashions that the season requires. If all goes well, we will tell her that she can have a permanent position. And when my sister goes to attend finishing school in Paris, Parthena may find herself a husband; we will help with introductions. How easy it will be to dazzle and bemuse her young feminine mind.' He smiled, hating the rogue he was portraying. Yet after years at war, a mere deception to a greedy fool was really neither here nor there on the scale of his sins. What was it compared to taking a life? Besides, this was in a very good cause.

'And will you do all this for her?' Bertram looked incredulously at him.

'No, of course not!' Jerome laughed. 'Why on earth would I? But she will believe it all. Therefore, when she willingly steps into my carriage, she will be filled with enthusiasm for an adventure in a very different and exciting world. You do not need to know any further details about what will befall her. I will send word that she has run off with some young dandy who turned her head or such, if you wish to hear anything; but a woman with such looks is always in demand in London, believe me.' He winked at Bertram, who was so eager to believe his problems had easily been solved that he would agree to any subterfuge Jerome suggested. If he could arrest the rogue then and there for his part in this make-believe scenario, Jerome thought bitterly, he would. In the process of saving Parthena, how satisfying it would be to see Bertram fall. He wondered if Stanton had made enquiries into Bertram's estate or affairs.

Bertram smiled. 'I do not need to know any more. I shall leave it all to your judgement.'

'Good! May I suggest I dine with you tonight, where we can persuade Miss Parthena that her future would be best served if she takes me up on my offer?'

'Yes, yes of course. Do you wish to stay the night?' Bertram asked, apparently quite taken by his cunning new friend.

'I am afraid I cannot, for I have a room in the town. But perhaps you could meet me in the coffee house tomorrow, say at a half past ten, and we can run through the details of when I should leave. That is, if the lady is willing. She must leave here happily, even if her happiness does not endure once she is in the city. I have my reputation to consider,' Jerome said with a smirk.

'Excellent idea. I will arrange for dinner, then. Do you wish to meet her now; soften her up a little?' Bertram winked at him.

'Excellent notion, Bertram! Perhaps she could show me the garden and the path by the river. I understand from Charles that the fishing is also excellent.' Jerome could not believe how easily Bertram had fallen into his trap. It was said that love was blind, but it seemed that greed was a much stronger blindfold to one's senses.

'Yes, give me a moment and I will ask her to make herself ready for a stroll.'

Bertram scuttled out of the study, which gave Jerome a chance to look around. He saw the large folder upon the desk and had a quick glimpse inside. It was clear from the plans and drawings inside that Charles was not interested in fishing, but rather the fast flow of the river and the position of the estate, which gave it a favourable aspect for the building of a mill. More than one building was planned, though; there was a manufactory also.

Stanton was correct: these plans would destroy the village. To save her home, Parthena had to marry, and sharpish. But would she? Persuading Bertram to 'trick' her was easy, but persuading her to marry him for the good of the village or to please his heart's desire could well be a momentous task. He could appear to be an opportunist who had learned the truth and wished to steal her birthright. Would she see that he genuinely adored her? He closed the file and sat back down in the chair, awaiting Bertram's return.

The man blustered in, shaking his head. 'Women! I shall never understand them, and am pleased to have escaped their grasp. I have no wish to have one pester me day and night. However, I will need an heir for my new estate soon enough.' He shrugged.

'Are you staying here, then?' Jerome asked, genuinely confused for a moment.

'No, no not this one! With the proceeds of our deal, I have plans to buy a property in Kent. Mama has always been desirous of land near Hythe, so perhaps we will be neighbours. Once the funds come through, I can make the dear lady's dream come true, and then it will be time to marry and think of an heir to carry on the Munro name.' He did not look happy at the prospect.

'You are planning quite an adventure yourself, it seems.'

'Yes, quite.'

Thena knocked on the door of the

study. 'Ah, there you are,' Bertram said. 'Could you show Mr Fender around the grounds, my dear? I shall watch you from the window, but I fear my gout is playing up again, and I must save myself for dinner.'

'Very well,' Thena answered. If she was trying to look less than enthusiastic, Jerome thought she was doing an excellent job of it.

'Thank you, Miss Munro.' Jerome stood up. 'I shall enjoy the gardens; and as for the fishing, I hear it is excellent.' He smiled and addressed Bertram. 'When we return, I shall go to the village and arrange for the coach and so on.'

'The coach?' Thena repeated as they walked to the main door.

'Yes, I intend to return to London for the season. My sister is so looking forward to it.' He was walking alongside Thena, who was paying him a great deal of attention. He hoped it would impress Bertram, who was following on behind, at least to the threshold. 'Tell me, Miss Munro have you seen Pall Mall or the gardens at Vauxhall?'

'Why no, Mr Fender, I have not. Would you care to tell me about them?' she asked as she stepped out and walked carefully down the steps to the path that ran around the old building to the main gardens behind to the river.

'Yes, of course,' Jerome said, and waited a moment before turning to Bertram and whispering to him, 'By the end of this week, you shall say goodbye to your cousin for good, and she you.'

Bertram slapped him on his back and chuckled. 'Good man,' he replied before shutting the door on them.

# 11

Thena was surprised by Bertram's request that she walk with Jerome alone around the grounds. If he had not whispered to her in the hallway previously, she would have doubted where Jerome's loyalties lay. He played his role, whatever it was, with complete and convincing confidence.

'So tell me, Mr Fender, what guise do you appear in today, using your own name, but having Bertram's agreement to our meeting — and in relative privacy?' She stopped at a rose and pointed to it as though discussing its colour or scent.

'I have simply come to him as myself, offering him my card and some help in solving a problem that I have recently become aware of.' He smiled politely at her as they walked and talked.

'What is that?'

'Why, you, of course. I overheard him talking with some of his associates in town, and have convinced him that I know his business partner and am a party to the knowledge that you stand in the way of them and their intentions. Since then, I have seen the plans in his study, and they indeed bode ill for the future of this beautiful place.'

'I have too. He will destroy everything here for the people. He will bring in many poor souls to work in his mill, and the village and the land will be changed forever. It galls me, as it seems there is nothing I can do about it, Jerome.' She looked up at him. 'I owe you so much already that I can never repay — but is there any way you can help me prevent him from carrying out his plans?'

'That is why I am here. I met an old colleague of mine, a man who was at the Inns when I was there.'

Thena looked at him and repeated, 'The inns? What inns? Did he see us?' Her mind reeled at the thought that someone in the village knew she had spent the night with Jerome.

'Not that kind of inn. The Inns of Court in London — The Middle Temple.'

'Oh,' she said, 'I see.' But she really did not.

'Come, walk and talk with me further. We must not arouse your cousin's suspicions.' They walked along with a foot or so between them, so that they did not touch even by accident.

'Mr Stanton trained where I did, at the same law school,' Jerome said. 'He is your family's legal representative, and speaks well of your father and the village. He has a gift for you from your father — a key, and I believe a letter for your twenty-first birthday, to be given to you along with the grandfather clock that he also left you. Stanton did not tell Bertram of this, not even when you disappeared. Bertram would have had him believe you had run away, Thena.'

'I *knew* my father must have left his affairs in order!' she said, filled with a rush of emotion. 'And I did no such thing — I would never run away!' She was appalled at how low Bertram would stoop to rid himself of her. What must Jerome be thinking of her and her corrupt cousin? She hoped beyond hope Jerome did not believe that a tendency to go to the bad was in her bloodline, and was therefore the reason why she had stolen from him. She could not help but smile slightly, though.

'What amuses you?' he asked.

'My dear father has left me time.' She looked up at the sun. 'That clock represents words of wisdom he once shared with me, and reminds me of how precious our time with loved ones is.' Then her smile faded. 'If only I had loved ones left to care . . . '

'Oh, Thena, he has left you precious little time. The will clearly leaves the estate to your cousin. The legacy of the land applies to it being kept as it is, if inherited through the direct line, but the wording is not specific enough. It stipulates what should happen if the estate is passed from father to son, or son-in-law; and also what happens next if it must go to the nearest male relative. However, because it was poorly prepared, the codicil of the land does not specify what happens if the only people in line to inherit are uncles, cousins, second cousins and so on.'

Jerome was trying to make this simple for her to understand, Thena knew that, but the unfairness of it all galled her. 'I was referring to the grandfather clock. It stopped some time ago, but Father always said that time was the most precious gift anyone can give — though his sadly ran out to soon. But if what you say is true, Bertram has won. I cannot stop this sale.'

They had stopped walking by the banks of the river. Jerome glared down at the water as if trying to see the fish. 'There is a way, Thena. But it requires a great sacrifice on your part, along with a willingness to trust me again.'

Thena looked at him: his face betrayed how serious he was. She could tell by the way his features moved that he was trying to find the words to explain his idea to her as simply and effectively as possible. How difficult could it be for a man of law to express his thoughts? she wondered; but then his words came back to her — 'or son-in-law' — and she swallowed. Was he really thinking of stepping in to rescue her again? Surely a man like Jerome already had a wife. But then he had been at war, and war is a destroyer of the normal order of life.

They walked along the river path a way, but stayed within view of the house, as they were both aware that they were being watched by Bertram.

'Thena, we have been thrown together in the most unlikely way, and yet I believe fate has had a hand in this. To stop Bertram and save your village, you need to be married by the end of this month. That is it in a nutshell.'

'It is impossible . . . '

'Hear me out, Thena. I do not wish to shock you . . . I know this is all very sudden, and must seem incredulous to you, but your cousin did not give you a chance, as he withheld the will's contents from your sight and knowledge.'

'No, Jerome; I mean it is impossible because the banns need weeks to be read, and — '

'That is only if you marry in the Church in England, Thena. But there is another, more daring, way. Have you heard of elopement to a place called Gretna Green?' Jerome looked at her and smiled. 'Scottish laws are different.'

'How would I get away, and whom would you suggest I marry — Mr Stanton?' She was trying hard not to change the way she walked, which was meant to look relaxed to Bertram.

'No. Anyway, he already has a wife. I am proposing to you, Thena. I would be delighted if you would agree to be my wife. I am suggesting that you and I go to Gretna Green and get a quick marriage licence, then return quickly to stop Bertram and save your village.' He looked away momentarily, pointed to some imagined object of interest, and then looked back at her.

She stopped and stared at him, Bertram momentarily forgotten. Jerome would do this for her?

'I find you beautiful and beguiling,' Jerome continued earnestly, 'and I would be happy for us to really get to know each other well. But that is up to you. How we would do this is simple. I am only acting like a total cad for the benefit of your cousin. I have offered to remove you to London. You need to look excited, Thena, as if I am selling you a dream of attending balls and being dressed in such finery that no head will be left unturned as you enter the assembly or gatherings. I am supposed to be dazzling you with the prospect of a chance to see society in all its glory and hypocrisy as part of this dream, and promising you that you will attend the finest events as a companion to my fictitious younger sister, Eleanor, who is lonely.'

Thena looked back at the river. This was a lot to take in. Could she trust Jerome? If she was his wife, he would be the heir of this estate and not Bertram. But she knew so little about him, and he knew all her darkest secrets. Could he be so genuine, so lovely, handsome and kind that he would truly forfeit his freedom for her?

'We have little time left, Thena. I am to dine here tonight, and you must be full of enthusiasm to meet 'Eleanor' and leave with me without a thought of looking back at this place. If you play this right and receive Stanton tomorrow at eleven, I will keep Bertram busy, and then within two days you will leave this place with me. But instead of heading south to my London residence, we will head north at speed to Gretna Green, and in that way we can stop the blackguard. Take heart — I have money and property and do not need to take advantage of your situation, but I have come to love this place and I would promise to protect it for generations to come from the likes of Tripp.'

He looked down at her with a great deal of what she saw as concern in his eyes. 'Thena, I know it is a very difficult decision for you; but if you do not do this, I have no hope of a happy future for you. Bertram, I believe, wishes you harm — he wants you cleared from his path. If I could arrest him for what he would *like* to do, then I would, and he would be hanged. But he has not committed the act yet, and it would break me to come so near to saving you, only to have lost the chance.'

'Jerome, next you will be declaring that you love me.' Thena looked away and laughed.

'Would that be so unpalatable?' he asked.

Thena was genuinely taken aback. He was either a very sensitive and genuine person, despite his rank and profession, or an extremely good actor.

She smiled brightly as they returned to the Hall. 'Very well,' she told him, 'if you are willing and sincere, then let our adventure continue, Mr Fender. Use whatever powers you have to protect my villagers, my home and my heart, and destroy the vermin that has taken up residence within it.' She did not wait for his reply, but stepped enthusiastically back into the Hall.

'You enjoyed your walk, Parthena?' Bertram greeted her.

'Very much so, cousin. I have much to tell you,' she said.

'Oh, good, good, but later. Mr Fender will join us for dinner and we shall talk then.'

'Very well, Bertram,' she responded, and passed by the grandfather clock. She smiled. Bertram's reign was about to come to an abrupt end.

When she returned to her room, Thena began to repack for a very different journey. This time she would not be facing a lonely life as a governess at some family's beck and call. No, she was going to marry a man whose purse she had stolen, she thought with a mental laugh, though she was beginning to believe she had unwittingly stolen his heart as well. The thought filled her with more hope and happiness than she had felt in a year. At the loneliest and most desperate time in her life, Jerome had appeared to her in the night as she had crossed a lonely street to find shelter behind an inn, hoping there was a stable she could hide in. Fate he had called it, but destiny was a better word, she thought.

# 12

The dinner had been very frustrating for Thena. She had wanted to ask Jerome so much about his life, his world, his family, but instead had had to endure an evening that felt more like a game of charades. Bertram asked many questions and, if Jerome answered honestly, he had property in London and an estate in Kent. Bertram almost drooled when Jerome mentioned Boodles and Almack's Assembly Rooms, the ton, and joked about it being 'the marriage mart' where he had met his own dear wife. He was planning on Eleanor stepping out there, as it was to be her first season. The smokescreen they created for Bertram worked, as he thought her senseless and witless, as she questioned Jerome about this ficticous sister and the life of a London lady as opposed to the life of a lady of the manor on a country estate. Bertram so believed that she was being duped by Jerome that it was comical and sad to behold such a fickle mind as his. Ironic really, Thena thought, as it was he who had been duped.

* * *

Mr Stanton arrived promptly. Thena was waiting near the door for him so that he did not need to alert the servants of his presence. These were strange times, so protocol was no longer something she worried about.

Once in the day room, she closed the doors behind them. 'So, Mr Stanton, I understand you have a gift for me from my father.'

'Yes, I have.' He promptly produced an envelope from his leather bag. 'This was for you for your twenty-first birthday, Miss Munro.'

'I thank you for keeping it safe for my eyes only.' Thena took it, then apologetically added, 'I have not offered you any refreshments.'

'There is no need, miss. I do not wish to be found here.' He smiled. 'Is there anything you would like me to assist you with before I leave, Miss Munro?'

'Yes, there is,' she replied, as she read the short note. It simply said: *Take care of your time, my dear Parthena, and use it wisely!*

'Then ask,' Geoffrey prompted her.

'Is Mr Jerome Fender a genuine and honest man?' She stared at him as she anxiously waited for his reply.

'I knew him some years ago, before the wars, but he was an honourable man whom I looked upon as a friend, with great admiration. I do not think you would find a better man, if I am honest, and I believe he has your best interests at heart.'

Thena was relieved to hear it, and judged this man to be honest as well, as he had kept her personal gift away from Bertram. 'Then please bear witness to my use of this key,' she said, 'as it opens the door in the clock's case.' They went out into the hall where it stood.

'It's a Dumbvile longcase,' Thena explained as she used the key to open the panel in its base. 'My father had this compartment specially made. He would keep what he called his emergency fund there.'

She crouched down and pulled out a velvet pouch and a leather wallet. 'Oh, look!' she said as she found an emerald ring, necklace and earrings. A piece of paper simply wished her well and to be proud of who she was. The wallet held notes to the value of two hundred pounds. 'This is a fortune!' she exclaimed.

One last document was the deed to the schoolhouse in the village. A further message was left with this, stating: *You will always have a home in Leaham, should you need it.*

'He left me the schoolhouse. The first floor of it has living quarters, and the attic is a study room that overlooks the salmon course and the river. He wanted me to have some independence if I was not married or welcome at the Hall. But for all his generosity, it is nowhere near enough to save the land from my cousin's plans. Please come with me, Mr Stanton, and I will show you the drawings in his study.'

When Geoffrey cast his eyes over them, a look of horror crossed his face. 'If this goes ahead, the village, and my home, will be ruined.' He stared at Thena.

'Unless I am married before the end of the month, to a man whom I can trust and who will help me foil Bertram's plan,' she said; but really it was a question to make sure that neither she nor Geoffrey had missed anything.

'Yes, that is so,' he confirmed.

'Then I will bid you good day, and when next we meet I will be a married lady.' She held her head up proudly as she replied.

'I wish you well, Miss Munro, and I thank you from the bottom of my heart.' Geoffrey's words drifted off as he made his way to the doorway of the Hall.

Thena watched him go, then gathered her things and summoned Mrs Hubbart. She had a journey to prepare for, and a future to secure.

* * *

It was after a very rushed trip, at speed, that the coach finally arrived outside the blacksmith's in Gretna Green. The thought of a church wedding with all the trimmings and a village celebration had lost its appeal to Thena, anyway, when her father died. The noise of the vehicle caused a rush of excitement in her it carried the two elopers on their way.

They took a breath of fresh air as they alighted from the coach. Holding on to each other, they steadied themselves as their arrival was made known.

'Thena, if you wish to change your mind, I will not hold it against you,'

Jerome said. 'But once we step through that door and are wed before an anvil, not an altar, it will be too late to regret your decision.'

'Are you sure it is not yourself who is having doubts?' Thena returned. 'It hardly compares with the kind of wedding your family would expect of you, would it?' She saw his face change. Shock, she thought, and her heart ached, for she was sure he *had* doubted his gallant but rash decision.

'Thena, I do not care what they expect. I do not want a marriage that is shallow. I want you! I want someone who feels passion for the land they represent, for the life they have, and hopefully in time for me. I do not wish to live in London. If you are willing, I would live at the Hall and learn how to strengthen the affairs of the estate so that it would never be threatened again. If you are willing, I want this to be a real marriage.'

'Oh, Jerome, I am more than willing, for that is what I desire also. But I do not deserve you.' She flung her arms around his neck. They kissed like true lovers, but he pulled away.

'We should seal our fate quickly, I think.' He was almost laughing as he spoke, but then a serious note returned to his voice. 'I forgot to tell you that, when we do this, we will not only stop Bertram Munro in his tracks, but we will bring the man low. He has debtors he will not be able to pay.'

Thena did not hesitate to reply. 'Then let him be brought low. He cared not for how many others' lives he would destroy to pay for his own lifestyle. He must be stopped!'

'Very well, then. Shall we, Miss Munro?' And he took her hand, ready to lead her into the blacksmith's shop, where the brief ceremony would be performed according to Scottish law.

'No regrets?' Jerome asked one last time before they crossed the threshold.

'None, Mr Fender, I promise,' Thena said, and stepped into her future.

*Books by Valerie Holmes*
*in the Linford Romance Library:*

THE MASTER OF MONKTON MANOR
THE KINDLY LIGHT
HANNAH OF HARPHAM HALL
PHOEBE'S CHALLENGE
BETRAYAL OF INNOCENCE
AMELIA'S KNIGHT
OBERON'S CHILD
REBECCA'S REVENGE
THE CAPTAIN'S CREEK
MISS GEORGINA'S CURE
CALEB'S FAITH
THE SEABRIGHT SHADOWS
A STRANGER'S LOVE
HEART AND SOUL
BETHANY'S JUSTICE
FELICITY MOON
THE VALIANT FOOL
TABITHA'S TRIALS
THE BAKER'S APPRENTICE
RUTH'S REALITY
LEAP OF FAITH
MOVING ON
MOLLY'S SECRET

CHLOE'S FRIEND
A PHOENIX RISES
ABIGAIL MOOR:
THE DARKEST DAWN
DISCOVERING ELLIE
TRUTH, LOVE AND LIES
SOPHIE'S DREAM
TERESA'S TREASURE
ROSES ARE DEAD
AUGUSTA'S CHARM
A STOLEN HEART
REGAN'S FALL
LAURA'S LEGACY